I dedicate this novel to my friends in the Oswestry Writing Group who have been so supportive over the years.

DAY ONE

ONE

As they bounced down a narrow lane across a flat, bleak landscape DI Dundee asked for the second time, 'What's this place?'

'Whixall Moss,' his colleague, DS Eccles, told him. She was hanging on grimly to the steering wheel as the car bucked over the ruts.

'Oh, I know all about moss. Right bloody nuisance! Ruining my lawn!'

'No, Jack, not that kind of moss. It's the name of the peat bog here. Stretches for miles. One of the largest peat bogs in the country. Apparently you can see it from space.'

'How do you know all this?'

'Did a course. The flora and fauna of north Shropshire. Went with Tricia. Before she moved on.'

'How's that new friend of yours? Sabine?'

This was the girl who'd identified the victim in a previous case they had been involved in. She had moved in with Eccles and become an interpreter for the police when dealing with the growing Polish community.

'She's fine.'

Dawn wasn't ready to tell him that Sabine had moved on as well. She had decided to return to Poland, now that things were improving over there. Dawn understood this, but was still broken hearted.

Jack looked around at the vast acres of open land.

'Does anybody live here? I haven't seen a house for ages.'

'Well apparently we're nearly there, according to the satnav. Lilac Cottage.'

'Lilac Cottage. Sounds nice. So fill me in, Dawn.'

'There's been a nasty murder.'

'Go on.'

'Local bobby phoned in about six this morning. Neighbour heard a scream. Phoned the police. When PC Blount got to the house, there was a man dead in the hallway. Back of his head bashed in. Wife and son distraught.'

'Break-in gone wrong?'

'Well that's one angle.'

Suddenly a short row of cottages came into view and the satnav told them they'd reached their destination. A flicker of sunlight broke through the low cloud and it was obvious which one was Lilac Cottage, because it had already been taped off.

They came to a halt near the fence, between two other police vehicles. Jack got out of the car and stood looking around. 'Long way to the shops,' he said and then he went into a sort of daydream until Dawn called to him.

'Jack!'

She was irritated by her partner's unfocussed attitude. He'd been like that for a while now, but she couldn't work out why. He was usually a good detective; very observant and quick to work things out, but just lately he kept slipping into this dreamy mode. He was far too young to be having senior moments: it was almost as if he was in love. Dawn had been his partner for a couple of years but, because of her sexual orientation, the partnership avoided the problems that a man and woman working together for long hours sometimes caused.

Both detectives had been highly commended for their recent success with the sex-trafficking case but the return of their much loved DCI from maternity leave had closed the door to promotion within the relatively small south Shropshire force. Dundee had been granted a transfer to the much larger force at Shrewsbury and Dawn had followed him. Jack's marriage seemed to be

3

secure again. His wife, Leanne, was happy with their move to Shrewsbury, with its wider range of shops and entertainments. She had soon found another job in a local hairdressing salon and the twins seemed to have settled well into their new school.

At last Jack came out of his reverie. PC Blount met them at the door of the cottage. Inside it was small but clean and cosy. Several scene of crime personnel in their paper suits and overshoes, were carefully checking the floor and a photographer was busy with the corpse. Blount explained that the police surgeon had been notified and was on his way.

He led them carefully past the dead man through to the kitchen where a pretty, blonde woman in her late thirties sat wrapped in a pink blanket. Beside her was a boy in his mid-teens. The woman was trembling and in tears. The boy, almost unhealthily thin, thought Dawn, sat in a very clean white T-shirt and pale blue jogging bottoms, very tense and pale. Both were holding cups of what looked like tea.. The boy had hardly touched his.

Jack showed his ID and introduced them both.

'Detective Inspector Dundee and Detective Sergeant Eccles. Can you please tell us your names?'

Dawn showed her card. The woman whispered between sobs, 'Julie. Julie Talbot. This is my son, Paul.' Then the sobbing grew louder as she added, 'Had his sixteenth birthday only yesterday.'

Simultaneously, mother and son both put down their cups.

Dawn wrote their names in her notebook. She thought the boy seemed tall for his age.

Jack went on, 'Look, I know this is a terrible time, but do you feel up to answering a few questions?'

The woman wiped her eyes with a tissue and nodded.

Eccles spoke to the boy. 'Would you like to leave us for a while? This won't be pleasant.'

'No. I'll stay with Mum. She'd prefer that.'

Of course correct procedure would have been to interview them separately, thought Dawn, but Jack didn't seem concerned. The woman took her son's hand in hers and gave a wan smile.

'Right,' said Dundee. 'Mrs Talbot. Julie. Tell us exactly what you remember.'

The woman paused, as if preparing a speech, then began. 'Something woke me early. Some sort of sound from downstairs. It took me a while to wake properly. I've been taking sleeping pills.'

'Did you recognise the sound?'

'I thought it was my husband...For a while I imagined I was dreaming. There was a thump, like someone or something falling over. Then it was quiet again. At first I thought my husband must have tripped over something on his way outside. The curtains were closed so it would still have been quite dark downstairs. He sometimes goes out in the garden early. To commune with nature, is how he puts it. He loves the natural world, you see.'

Eccles noticed a smirk on the boy's face as his mother said this. Then Mrs Talbot put her hand to her mouth.

'Oh, I keep talking as if poor Bernard was still alive.'

The woman paused briefly, and went on.

'By now I was properly awake so I got out of bed and started to go down but Paul met me on the stairs. He told me to stay where I was. Something terrible had happened. He's such a good boy. Really looks after me.'

The woman leant across and put her head on the boy's shoulder. Eccles noticed a small bruise on the woman's neck, before she pulled the blanket round her again. Surely that was a love-bite. Was incest involved? God help us, thought Eccles. Or

5

was she having an affair? Was that why the murder had happened?

The boy took his mother's other hand in his and squeezed it.

Jack turned to the boy. 'When did you see what had happened to your father?'

'I was half awake anyway, thinking about my GCSEs, which are coming up soon. I thought I heard someone moving about downstairs. I got up and hurried down. It was still dark and I knocked over a chair. That's what must have woken Mum. Then I saw Dad lying in the hallway, with a trickle of blood seeping from his head. I knew at once that he was dead. I couldn't help crying out.'

Mrs Talbot gave a little gasp, and sobbed again.

'Was there anyone else downstairs?'

'No, but I thought I heard a click and saw the back door close. I ran to look, but there was no one there. There's a little copse at the back of our garden, so it would be easy to disappear. I started to go back upstairs and met Mum coming down. I told her not to come any further, but she'd already seen Dad and she screamed and screamed. I thought she was going to faint so I helped her to the kitchen and went upstairs for a blanket to wrap round her. I was just making tea for us both when there was a knock on the door. It was Mr Briggs, our neighbour. He lives in the end cottage, number four. He told us not to touch anything and he went back to his cottage to call the police. He didn't have a mobile and he wouldn't use our phone.'

DS Eccles wrote 'Briggs. Number 4' in her notebook.

The boy turned to his mother. The colour had returned to his face.

'Have I forgotten anything, Mum?'

There was a pause. Then DI Dundee asked, 'Mrs Talbot, can you think of anyone who would want to harm your husband?'

'Well he wasn't universally popular, but who is?'

As the woman spoke Eccles noticed another secret smile cross the boy's face.

'And the nature of his work meant that he antagonised some of the local farmers and businessmen. I mean no one likes to be told they must stop doing something they enjoy doing, like hunting for instance, or fighting with dogs.'

'But surely,' Eccles said, 'those things were banned ages ago.'

'Well, some people round here don't think that laws like that apply to them. You see my husband took a very moral stance. But I can't think anyone would go as far as to kill him for his point of view.'

There was a knock on the door and one of the scene-of-crime team came to tell them that the police surgeon had arrived.

DI Dundee asked the mother and son to stay in the kitchen while the surgeon examined the victim.

'Perhaps DS Eccles will make you another cup of tea.'

Dawn scowled with the thought that Jack was using her as a skivvy but assumed that he was just being thoughtless and took the used cups to the sink. Jack closed the kitchen door and walked back to the hallway where the police surgeon was kneeling beside the corpse.

TWO

Jones, the police surgeon, was short, plump and Welsh. He was quite young, with a large round head, a mop of black curls and a vigorous black beard. He ordered the SOCOs and the photographer out of the hallway, so that he could examine the corpse. As he moved around the body he made little sounds, sometimes words in English like, 'Yes…yes' or snatches of Welsh and sometimes he whistled a few notes of a song. He was like a kettle bubbling away, about to boil.

DI Dundee waited patiently for the doctor to finish his examination. At last the young man stood still and silent and closed his eyes. When he opened them again he almost jumped at the sight of Jack, as if he hadn't noticed him before. Then he murmured, 'Nasty. Nasty,' paused then asked, 'You are?'

'Detective Inspector Dundee. Recently transferred to north Shropshire. I don't think we've met.'

'No. Heard of you though. That sex-trafficking business.' He offered his rubber gloved hand. 'Aled Jones.'

Dundee declined the hand but said cheerfully, 'Pleased to meet you.'

Jones remembered that his hand had recently examined a bloody skull and withdrew it. He smiled broadly. Jack was reminded of a stone Buddha in a neighbour's garden. He liked the young doctor's friendliness and obvious energy. So different to the dour, cynical Clarke, close to retirement, with whom he'd worked in south Shropshire.

'OK,' said Dundee. 'What can you tell me about the vic?'

'Male. Caucasian. A hundred and eighty-three centimetres. That's about six foot two in old money. Mid to late thirties. Good physique. Looks reasonably fit and healthy, well, for a corpse.'

'Cause of death?'

'Severe trauma to the parietal region of the skull. In layman's terms...a bloody great thump to the back of the head.'

'Weapon?'

'Heavy, solid, probably metal. The wound is deep but fairly narrow. My guess would be a hammer. Be more specific when we've got him on the slab.'

'Do you think he was killed here?'

'Well that's a bit of a poser. From the way he's lying it looks as if he was trying to reach the front door to get away from his attacker. But there's very little blood and rigor has begun to set in. Time of death? My guess would be about two hours ago.'

Jack thought about that timing. It didn't tie in with what Mrs Talbot and her son had told them.

'Strange. Anything else?'

'Well, the blow was probably administered by someone at least as tall as the victim.'

'Someone pretty strong?'

'Not necessarily. The way a hammer's designed it does most of the work itself. You just swing it and hey presto! If you're tall enough that is. Even a woman could do it.'

Dundee murmured, 'Hmm,' and thought about the pretty young widow in the kitchen, who was certainly not tall. Then he asked, 'Would you expect there to have been a lot of blood?'

'Yes, anyone in range would have been spattered.'

Dundee 'ummed' again and thought about the boy in his clean white T-shirt and immaculate blue trousers.

'Well, what else can you tell me?'

'If you could help me turn him over, we'll have a look at his face. If we both move that arm gently...'

The face revealed was ghastly. The man had died of shock. His blonde hair was quite long. He had a small blonde moustache and his mouth was open in a hideous grin.

'A good set of gnashers. Looked after his diet I reckon.'

Dundee tried to avoid sarcasm as he said, 'So, a victim with a broken skull and good teeth. Thanks, Doc. That's all very helpful.'

Just then Jack noticed that the fingers of the hand they had just revealed were clutching a small wild flower, with its petals unopened.

Jones noticed it too.

'Strange that. Surely he wasn't killed for picking wild flowers.'

'No, but please make sure it's bagged and goes to the mortuary along with the corpse.'

'Will do.'

'I'm used to having to screw every nugget out of the surgeon at my last place.'

'Sorry to hear that. After all we're both on the same side. Oh, and don't call me Doc. Aled will do. We're likely to meet fairly often, now you're in this neck of the woods. You are?'

'Jack.'

'OK, Jack, I'll make sure we have some photographs of this side, then we'll get this unfortunate chap off to the mortuary.'

Jones went to speak to the photographer and Dundee walked through the living room deep in thought.

The back door was open and one of the scene of crime team was dusting the frame for fingerprints.

Dundee whispered. 'When you've finished in here, start a search outside. We're looking for an implement, a hammer or something like, and possibly some bloodstained clothing. Have a look in the wheelie bin.' As he spoke he realised what a stupid thing he'd said. No self-respecting murderer would choose such an obvious place.

The officer nodded and went to speak to the Crime Scene Manager. Dundee went into the kitchen. Eccles sat at the table with the woman and her son. Both seemed more relaxed now. Eccles stood up and put her cup and saucer in the sink. She seemed eager to be on her way.

'Right,' said Dundee, watching mother and son for their reaction as he said, 'The ambulance will be arriving soon to take your husband's body to the mortuary.'

The woman raised a tissue to her eyes as if to wipe away a tear. The boy took his mother's hand and held it tight.

Jack continued, 'DS Eccles and I will be speaking to Mr Briggs and your other neighbours. Someone might have seen an intruder. Our lot will probably be here all day. This is now a crime scene. So for today you must stay in the kitchen. Is there anyone nearby you could stay with for a while? Member of the family perhaps? Or a friend? Or I could arrange for a Victim Support Officer to come and stay here with you.'

It was the boy who answered. 'No thank you. Mum and I will be fine.'

Eccles looked at Mrs Talbot. 'Are you sure?' The woman – a widow now – nodded and gave a half smile. 'My family live a long way away. I don't really have friends here. They were always Bernard's friends.'

'Obviously we shall need to speak to you again,' said Dundee. 'I'll be sending someone out to take a proper statement from you later today. Oh, and Doctor Jones is here, if you'd like something to...'

Neither the widow nor her son looked as if they needed any help from a doctor, so the detectives left the room. An ambulance had just arrived and the corpse was being lifted onto a stretcher. On their way out of the cottage Dundee spoke to the Crime Scene Manager.

'Anything?'

'We've started on the garden. But nothing yet. I'll be in touch if we find something.'

THREE

Lesia checked her phone again. She hadn't heard it buzz to tell her there was a message. But she may have missed it with the hubbub in the room. Most of the group had arrived by now and were filling the classroom, chattering away and preparing for their tour. Even on this cold February morning they would enjoy their introduction to the Moss because Bernard was such an interesting guide. But where the hell was he?

She'd had a crush on Bernard ever since her days at the Sixth Form College in Birmingham, where he had taught Environmental Science. But she had been far too shy to make her feelings known. Then just as she was preparing for her exams Bernard suddenly left the college. She was distraught; both as a pupil because he was such an excellent teacher, and as a young woman because her heart beat faster every time he came near.

It wasn't that he was particularly good looking; tall, well made, as her mother would say, with a mop of unruly fair hair and a little moustache. But it was his eyes that you noticed, piercingly blue, shining with intelligence and a passion for the natural world. Lesia had guessed he was in his thirties. She had seen him once in a local shopping centre with his pretty wife and teenage son. But this had not put her off.

Using the internet she discovered that Bernard had become a warden at some nature reserve in the sticks. Best to forget him and concentrate on her A levels. She did well in her exams and was all set to go on to university, when she saw an advertisement on the laboratory noticeboard for a trainee with the Shropshire Wildlife Trust. She applied, not really knowing where Shropshire was or what it was like, but simply because she knew that was where Bernard was now. Her parents were against the idea, partly because she was so young but also because she was black, and they had an idea that there wouldn't be many other black people in Shropshire. Eventually their daughter persuaded them with the promise that if she did not like the job she would leave at the end of the year and continue her studies.

Lesia was an only child and her parents had always been supportive. They agreed that if she got the job they would help her rent a small flat in Shrewsbury.

The day of the interview arrived. Lesia took the train to Shrewsbury and discovered, from the little map on her phone, that the wildlife centre was just an easy walk away. She liked what she saw of the town as she walked down a steep hill lined with half-timbered buildings, which were mostly posh shops. The people walking up or down the hill were mainly white, and they all looked well-off, which was certainly not the case where she lived. Lesia began to wonder if she would be able to fit in.

At last she reached the bottom of the hill and crossed a bridge over a wide, lazily flowing river, which she saw on the map was the River Severn. She walked under a railway bridge and saw in front of her a large, old church. Then she saw the sign for the wildlife centre on her right.

At the centre she found that there were three other candidates for the post, all girls. The interviews would not begin for half an hour so the girls chatted and Lesia soon discovered that the others were probably better qualified for the post: each one of them had lived in the countryside and had first-hand experience of the local animals and plants. Lesia had only known the streets of Birmingham, but she had always loved the park where her father had helped her to identify the different trees, and the birds who visited their tiny garden were another interest.

The candidates were told that they would be interviewed in alphabetical order, so Lesia Williams resigned herself to waiting anxiously for her turn. At last she was called into the interview room. There were three members on the appointment panel and to her surprise one of them was Bernard. She was shocked but tried not to show it. He seemed not to remember her and the interview proceeded in the usual way and she did well enough. Then she returned to the waiting area.

Suddenly Bernard appeared and asked her to accompany him to an office down the corridor, while another member of the panel spoke to the other candidates.

Bernard asked Lesia to sit down. He had been astonished at how she had changed in the year or so since he'd last seen her. In fact if he had not had her CV in front of him he might not have recognised her. He remembered this shy little thing from the college, who seemed to have no confidence or dress sense and who lowered her head every time he came near her. Now there was this well-dressed, self-possessed young woman, with her soft brown complexion and her pretty face framed with curtains of glossy black hair.

When he told her that she had impressed the panel and they would like to offer her the post a smile lit up her face and she became very attractive indeed.

FOUR

Most of the gardens in front of the cottages were full of dormant plants waiting for the spring sun to bring them to life, but the fourth one, where they were headed, was quite different. No fence and simply a square of pebbles, carefully raked, not even a weed to be seen.

When they knocked on the door it was opened immediately by a man, probably in his sixties, well built, immaculately dressed, with greying hair cut short and a bushy moustache neatly trimmed.

'Mr Briggs?'

'That's me. S'pose you're the detectives? Dreadful business. Poor Julie. Such a lovely woman. And married to that dreadful man.'

His voice was a sort of throaty growl. Jack and Dawn introduced themselves and showed their identity cards, which Briggs carefully inspected before standing aside and ushering them in. As they entered the cottage Dawn noticed that it was as clean and tidy as the man himself. He took them through to the kitchen and offered coffee, which Eccles – full of recent tea – refused but Dundee accepted. The detectives sat at the kitchen table while Briggs busied himself with kettle, instant coffee and cups. Dawn noticed how upright the man stood, which added a few inches to his moderate stature. She wondered if he'd once been in the army.

'So,' began Dundee, 'you were first on the scene next door, Mr Briggs. What did you see?'

'Yes. I'm an early riser. Always have been. Used to take the dog for a walk about half past five but since poor Bruno went to that kennel in the sky I just get dressed and mooch about. So I heard the screams. Not for the first time I might add.'

16

'Oh,' the detectives said in unison.

'Oh yes,' said Briggs, shaking his head.

They waited for more detail but none came.

'I knocked but no one answered so I opened the door which was not locked – strange that – and nearly fell over the body in the hallway. It was obvious he was dead. Hole in the back of his head and a trickle of blood on the floor. I was a bit shocked but I'd seen dead bodies before. Falklands. Northern Ireland...'

So he was in the army, thought Eccles.

'Mrs Talbot, er Julie, sweet little thing, and that odd lad of hers were just standing on the stairs hugging one another. I told them not to move anything, then I came back here and phoned your lot. Don't have a mobile. Can't bear the bloody things. When I returned next door they were sitting in the kitchen. She was very pale and a bit shaky. She'd got a blanket round her and they were drinking tea. I thought of offering a nip from my flask, which I usually carry with me, but I know she doesn't drink and he's too young. But they seemed all right so I went back outside and waited until young Blount arrived. Know him well. I'm a Magistrate you see.'

'How well did you know the victim?'

'Only too well. Arrogant bastard! Oh I know you shouldn't speak ill, etcetera...but I couldn't stand the man. A green snob he was. Always going on about global warming and telling me what I should or shouldn't do. Worked for that Wild Life lot... Bloody interferers. Waste of taxpayers' money if you ask me. You know the sort of guff. Don't use peat on the garden. It takes thousands of years to form. But what's the point of it if you can't put it on the garden?'

Dawn didn't think Briggs' front garden would be much improved with peat but perhaps the back garden was different.

'Caught me sticking a bottle in the bin one day. Gave me a lecture about recycling.'

Dundee had some sympathy with that. Leanne was a stickler for recycling. And the twins watched him like hawks. Probably heard about it at school.

'Then I discovered that he was hurting Julie. Yes, I knew what was going on. I could have killed...Oh, not quite the thing to say in the circumstances, eh.'

'So you didn't kill him?' asked Dundee.

'Me! Kill someone! Never! Well, except in the line of duty of course. But the way he treated that lovely little wife of his made my blood boil.'

'Did you see anyone else about?'

'Well, now that you ask, I think I did see someone, just before the screaming started. Only a brief glimpse mind you. I know it was a man, but I couldn't describe him. It was quite misty at the time. We get that morning mist a lot out here. But I remember he was walking quickly away from the houses and into those trees at the back. Thing is, I'm not sure which cottage he'd come from.'

'Can you show us exactly where he disappeared into the trees? Eccles, can you go with Mr Briggs and I'll have a word with Davies, the scene of crime manager. He'll have to scour that area as well.'

So Eccles accompanied Briggs towards the trees. He hesitated, then pointed to a small gap between two silver birch trees, where a well-trodden narrow path led out onto the Moss.

'About here, I reckon,' said Briggs.

Eccles saw Dundee approaching them with Davies at his side. The scene of crime manager hung some tape from tree to tree.

'I'll send a couple of the lads out to have a look,' said Davies. 'But don't get your hopes up, Jack.'

Davies walked back to the house. Briggs led them to a gate in his back fence and into his own garden, which was as barren and featureless as the front. There was a good deal of gravel and a few small flower beds, edged with perfectly placed bricks, and a large shed, recently repainted.

As they went back inside, Dundee asked, 'Do you live here on your own, Mr Briggs?'

'Oh yes. The wife died a while back.'

'And now you fend for yourself?'

'No problems there. Always could look after myself.'

'Thank you, Mr Briggs,' said Dundee. 'Of course we'll need you to make a proper statement later on.'

'I'll be here all day. No bus on Thursdays. And my car's being serviced in Ellesmere'

'Well thank you for your help, Mr Briggs. Oh, and please don't go talking to Mrs Talbot or her son just yet.'

'That's fine. I know the procedure.'

'Now we need to have a word with your other neighbours.'

Briggs smiled. 'Wish you luck there. Old Perry's deaf as a post and his missus is doolally. Lived here since the Ice Age. And the other lot, well they're foreigners. Don't know where from. But I wouldn't trust them further than I could throw them.'

FIVE

The people in the room were beginning to fidget. They had finished their drinks and washed up their cups. Some were sitting at the discarded school desks, which acted as tables in the room, studying the material Bernard had prepared for the day's course. The younger ones were checking their phones. Others were putting on coats and scarves or changing their shoes for walking boots or wellingtons. Lesia had warned them that the Moss could be very cold and wet at this time of the year. Increasingly they glanced at their watches, then at Lesia, waiting for an explanation. At last she said, 'I do apologise. I'm sure Mr Talbot will be here very soon.'

In the year since her interview at the wildlife centre Lesia had learned a great deal. At first she had worked in the centre, doing mundane office stuff or serving at the information desk, but whatever she did she did well and she was soon given more responsibility. Apart from a few racists, which you found everywhere, the public responded to her lovely smile and her increasing knowledge of the varied Shropshire habitats.

Lesia had found a place to live, in a nearby suburb, sharing with another girl, who worked at a local estate agents. Katie was engaged to a trainee solicitor called Simon. Lesia was not so sure about his feelings towards her. Katie was so immersed in life with her fiancé that she didn't have much time to share with Lesia, but that didn't matter because by now Bernard had asked her to become his assistant at the Moss centre. He picked her up each day and as they drove out to Whixall he told her all about this very special environment until she became equally fascinated by the place.

She didn't actually lecture the groups, but she supported them in recording their observations: she helped anyone who was elderly or disabled; she gave the health and safety announcements; she organised the dispersal into smaller groups; she made sure that everyone had what they needed. In fact she rapidly became Bernard's right-hand woman. He often wondered how that shy schoolgirl of a year or two back had become this confident young woman. But she never told him that the main cause had been a guy called Darren.

She supposed it was on the rebound from Bernard's disappearance that Lesia got into bad company. She started dressing in a more provocative way, had her hair styled, used more make-up, went clubbing and drinking alcohol, even tried smoking a little dope, and got involved with a group of black kids who liked a bit of fun. One of these was Darren. He was not all bad. For a start he had a job. But when he wasn't working he liked to let off steam. He was a fit, good looking young man, and Lesia's street cred went sky high when she was with him.

So a more confident, outgoing Lesia emerged from her chrysalis and for a while everything went well, until Darren wanted to take their relationship further. Lesia wasn't ready for sex. Darren wanted it all the time. So in the end she began to back off. Darren couldn't take that. He began to pester her. Then she saw the job in Shrewsbury. This would be a good way out. She didn't tell Darren when she went for the interview. In fact she told no one except her parents. Then she went to live in Shrewsbury and she hoped that Darren would become a thing of the past.

But it didn't work like that. Somehow or other he discovered where she'd gone and he followed her. He found out where she lived and began to visit. Lesia made it clear that she didn't want him there, but he persisted, so in the end Simon had to frighten him off, by telling him that he was a solicitor and he would go to the police and get a restraining order. Soon after that Simon got beaten up walking along the riverbank on his way to see Katie. It may not have been Darren, but Simon went to the police, and Darren's visits ceased.

There was a tension in the shared house for a while. Simon suggested that Katie should ask Lesia to leave but she wouldn't do that. At last things began to settle down again.

Lesia continued to work with Bernard and everything seemed fine, but one day Darren turned up at the wildlife centre and demanded to know where Lesia was. He said he was her brother and unfortunately the staff believed him, simply because he was black, and told him where she was. Darren looked the place up on his phone, borrowed a motorbike from a friend and made his way to the Moss centre.

Darren arrived just as the day's session had ended and the course members had gone home. Lesia and Bernard were sitting close together at one of the desks while Bernard explained the next day's activities. Suddenly Darren burst in and tried to drag Lesia away. Bernard may have looked pale and willowy but he kept himself fit and his first punch knocked Darren to the ground. As he rubbed his sore fist Bernard asked, 'Is this a friend of yours, Lesia?'

'He used to be. Now he's just a damn nuisance.'

'I'm afraid I'll have to ask you to leave, Mr er...'

Darren got his feet and shook his head. He turned to Lesia.

'Is this guy messing with you, Lesia.'

'I work with Mr Talbot. He's the tutor here. You have no right...'

'You mean you like this streak of piss?'

In the meantime Bernard had picked up his phone to call the police.

Darren left the room. They heard a motorbike rattling away at speed.

Lesia found she was trembling. Bernard enfolded her in his arms to comfort her. She hugged him close and let him kiss her.

SIX

When the detectives knocked at the third cottage a tall, trim elderly man came to the door.

'Mr Perry?' asked Dawn in a loud voice. 'I'm DS Eccles and this is my colleague DI Dundee.'

'Tom Perry. Aye that's me. No need to shout.'

Dundee frowned, as he showed his card.

'Mr Briggs said you were deaf.'

'I am when I choose to be. And I choose to be when the Major's wittering on. I takes my hearing aid out. Anyway, come in.'

They followed the man into the living room, which had a strange sweet smell, which Dawn recognised from the nursing home where one of her aunts had lived since her last stroke. She tried not to show her distaste.

'You called him "The Major",' said Dundee.

'That's what he calls himself, but I'd be surprised if he was ever more than an NCO.'

'He also suggested that your wife had dementia.'

'Aye, well, there's some truth in that, I'm sorry to say. My Margery was the sweetest, prettiest thing till a few years back. But now she struggles even to remember who I am. Anyway, that's not what you came to talk about, is it?'

'No,' said Eccles. 'Are you aware of what's happened next door?'

'Not really, except there's police everywhere. Has there been a burglary?'

'There's been a murder. Mr Talbot has been killed.'

Perry went pale. There was a silence. Then he said, 'Well that's a real shocker. Did she kill him? I knew they wasn't getting on too well. But murder!'

'We don't know who killed him. That's what we're trying to find out.'

'How well did you know Mr and Mrs Talbot?' Dundee asked.

'They've only been here a year or so. Keeps themselves to themselves. But in a place like this you can't avoid saying "Good morning" or "How are you?" She were a bit strange. Ignored Margery, like she couldn't cope with her problems. And the boy's weird. But I grew to like Bernard. Well, respect him anyway.'

They heard a woman call from upstairs.

'You'll have to excuse me for moment. The missus is in the loo. I'll try to get her back into bed till we've finished.'

Poor man, thought Dawn. She had been watching Tom while they'd been talking and she thought him a fine man. Must be in his seventies but had the build of a much younger man. Slightly stooped perhaps, as tall men often were. His full head of hair was silvery and rather long, but it looked right for his strong features and weather-beaten face. She felt his sincerity and warmth. Such a pity that his wife...

They heard a toilet flush, and a tap run, followed by a low conversation. Then Tom Perry came back downstairs.

Dundee got the interview going again.

'How long have you lived here, Mr Perry?'

'Oh, just about forever. Since Marg and me was married. Call me Tom by the way.'

'Fine, Tom. I'm Jack and this is Dawn.'

'Y'see I were a peat cutter. All the folk in these cottages were the same in those days. Bloody hard work it were an' all. Everything by 'and. Out on the Moss in all weathers. Then they started draining the Moss and brung in them machines. Huge great things they were. Could cut as much peat in an hour as we could in a day. Soon all the moss was drying out, changing the place completely. And loads of trees got planted. Then this conservation lot came in and stopped the digging. We was all made redundant.'

Tom took a pipe out of his pocket.

'Mind if I smoke?'

Jack and Dawn both shook their heads, so Tom lit up.

That pipe really suits him, thought Dawn and she quite liked the smell. So different from cigarettes. Tom continued.

'At first I was angry with that lot who'd caused me to lose my job. But I was getting on a bit. Mid-nineties that would have been. So I weren't far off retiring anyway. And they gave us some compensation.'

'You say you respected the dead man.'

'See, I were turnin' the gardin' over one day and he come to the fence for a chat. It were obvious he loved this place. The Moss, I mean. Asked me all sort of questions about the early days. And he knew more about the plants an' that than me, though I've lived here all m' life.'

'So you became friends?'

'No, not exactly friends, but we chatted now and then. He told me how much he loved his job. Gave up a better-paid job in Brum to become a warden. Mind you he never seemed to be short of money. Have you seen his car? Must have got it with the job. Brung his family out 'ere. But they don't like it at all. Think that was part of the problem between them.'

'Problem?'

'Ah, shouting and such. She looks all sweetness and light but by God she's a nasty tongue when she gets going. And that lad of hers is a bit odd.'

Jack's eyebrows shot up with surprise at the thought of that pretty young woman next door using bad language. Dawn noted that this was the second time the son had been called odd or weird. Obviously both the boy and his mother were going to have to be interviewed again, separately and much more thoroughly.

There came a tapping noise from upstairs and the querulous voice of a woman calling out something.

Tom said, 'Look, sorry, I'll have to go and see to her.'

Dawn nodded. 'Yes, of course. You all right with that, Jack?'

Dundee muttered one of his 'Hmms'. He seemed far away in thought.

The detectives got up to leave. Jack said, 'Just one more question, Tom. What time were you up this morning?'

'About seven. I sleeps much later since Margery...I gets very tired looking after her...Why?'

'I wondered if you'd heard or seen anything unusual.'

'No, but these walls'm quite thick and curtains would have been closed at that time. Oh, and my hearing aid wouldn't have been in then. Sorry, not much 'elp am I?'

'Oh, yes,' said Dawn. 'You've given us a lot to think about. Thanks, Tom.'

Tom went upstairs shaking his head and muttering, 'Murder! Bloody 'ell.'

The detectives let themselves out.

SEVEN

The group had now been waiting almost half an hour for their tour of the Moss. They were a mix of retired people and younger ones, probably unemployed, looking to add to their CVs. There was no heating in the room and they were getting cold and bored. Lesia looked at her watch again. In the end she decided to phone Bernard but his phone was dead. Suddenly she decided what to do.

'I don't know why but Mr Talbot has been delayed. I suggest we make a start. I know where he was going to take you, and when he does arrive he'll know where to find us.'

She watched as they all relaxed and got ready to go. She led them outside.

She locked the classroom and made her way, with the group, past some outbuildings, down a muddy track and into a copse. When they reached a clearing she stopped them, as she knew that Bernard would have done.

'Now, look carefully at the ground. What can you see?'

There was a moment's silence, then one of the young men said, 'A load of mud.'

This brought some desultory laughter. Lesia knew that she must assert her authority because she was young, female and black, but before she could say anything one of the older men spoke. 'There's piece of iron in the ground here. Bit rusty of course.'

The woman with him, possibly a daughter, too young for a wife, thought Lesia, added, 'Oh yes. And look, there's more there.'

Gradually the whole group became aware of the iron rails, about two feet apart, going both ways along a level causeway, sometimes hidden by the grass and with some bits missing altogether. Lesia tried not to sound patronising as she said, 'Well spotted. That's part of the old trackway. They used to load the peat onto waggons here and horses would pull them along this track to the railway which used to run somewhere over there.'

Lesia pointed in an easterly direction, where the rails ran off into the trees.

Just then the sun went in and the wind rose.

'Come on,' said Lesia. 'Let's keep walking before the rain starts.'

Their path left the old railway at right angles and grew wider. On either side there were deep ditches full of black water. At least the trees here protected them from the wind.

Suddenly the path came out into the open, where the trees had been cleared. A wide flat landscape stretched far away to a dark wall of conifers in the distance. Now there was no shelter from the chill February wind.

One of the group, a younger man, sidled up to her and said, 'You must really feel the cold after where you come from.'

Lesia could hardly believe what she was hearing, but she replied politely, 'Well, it can be pretty cold in Birmingham too.'

She called the group together. They stood close as if huddling to keep warm. A fine rain began to fall. She had to lighten the mood. Then she remembered Bernard's party trick.

'I want you all to jump up and down.'

'Is this to get us warm?' someone asked.

'Just try it.'

One or two of them did, especially a more extrovert older woman, dressed in a pink mackintosh and pink furry boots, who made a real effort, then exclaimed, 'Wow! It bounces!'

Gradually they all joined in and scowls were replaced by smiles as the earth beneath their feet went up and down, like a reluctant trampoline.

While they bounced and chuckled Lesia went to the side of the path, took off her gloves, put her hands in a pool of that dark brown water and pulled out a handful of bright green weed, which dripped water as she held it out.

'Now watch.'

After the bouncing she had their attention. She squeezed the green weed and an amazing amount of water came out of it.

'This is sphagnum moss. It holds water like a sponge. This whole area is covered with the stuff. When it's left for thousands of years it gradually turns to peat. The problem is that when people realised how useful peat could be they started to dig it up and the Moss began to drain.'

The rain had stopped. A tall man at the back of the group pointed into the sky, where a large bird was wheeling, sharply outlined against the grey cloud.

'Oh yes,' said Lesia. 'The buzzards love it here. They can easily spot their prey on this open land. But there are also curlews, skylarks and meadow pipits on the Moss, and lots of other birds.'

At that moment the buzzard swooped swiftly earthwards and some poor creature probably met an untimely end.

She told them about the other plants and animals of the Moss such as the bog mosses, cotton sedges, the cranberries and the insect-eating sundews. The course would run one day a month for four months, so they would see the plants that flowered later in the year. Later in the classroom she hoped Bernard would show them his pictures of some of the insects, such as the white -faced darter dragonflies and the raft spiders. She heard the group gasp when she told them about the adders which lay coiled in the sun later in the year, but even now they should stick to the way-marked paths, just in case.

Looking out across the desolate Moss one of the younger men, who was hugging the pretty girl next to him, asked, 'So they used to dig this peat stuff up from here. What for?'

'Fuel mainly. To heat their houses and cook their food.'

Someone else said, 'And that was bad for the Moss?'

'Well it wasn't so bad when it was only dug up by hand, but when they brought in machines and took loads away, it began to destroy the Moss. The peat dried out and trees began to grow. It changed the whole nature of the place.'

As she spoke her next words she thought of Bernard's earnest face and the passion in his voice.

'Since the digging stopped, we've begun to cut back the trees and dam the ditches to let the Moss begin to go back the way it was. Of course it will take years and years.'

The cold wind rose again and she pulled her coat around her.

'Come on. Let's go a bit further, before the next shower.'

As the group moved on towards the middle of this vast open plain, Lesia told them about the ancient bodies that had been found in the peat. The acidic water had preserved the flesh and hair remarkably well, even though the bones inside were dissolved away. Lesia had only seen these bodies in photographs, which Bernard had showed her, but she remembered them well.

As she walked along she kept glancing back in hope of seeing his tall thin frame hurrying to catch them up. What on earth had happened to him?

She tried to remember all the things he would have told them about the history of the place. She explained how it had been used to train soldiers in the First World War before they went off to the trenches in France. And how the bombers in the Second World War had used the Moss to practise dropping their bombs before flying off to demolish those cities, like Dresden and Hamburg, in revenge for the bombing of our cities and in an attempt to demoralise the German people.

The rain began again, heavier this time, and she thought they ought to get back to the classroom, but just as they turned, someone who had wandered away from the group called in an urgent way, 'Miss!'

Lesia smiled at being addressed in this way, then asked, 'Yes?'

A very earnest middle aged man, peering through his wet glasses, said, 'I thought you said no one was allowed to dig up the peat any more.'

'That's right.'

'So what's this then?'

Lesia hurried over to see what he was pointing at. The others followed. When she reached the man she saw that at the side of the path a hole had been dug about the size and shape of a grave and the peat had been dumped at the side. When she moved closer to investigate she suddenly stopped and screamed. Water had begun to seep into the trench but beneath its surface it was still possible to distinguish the features of a very human corpse.

EIGHT

The weather broke as Dundee and Eccles drove along the winding, uneven road towards the little market town of Wem, on their way back to Shrewsbury. Rain drummed on the roof and poured down the windscreen like a carwash. Eccles found it difficult to see the road ahead, even with the wipers going full throttle. Soon the many potholes on the narrow road were full and the wheels sent dirty water up in waves.

DS Eccles slowed down and turned on dipped headlights.

'I wouldn't fancy being out in this,' she said.

Dundee didn't respond. He seemed to be miles away. Suddenly he spoke.

'Right. Who d'you fancy for it?'

'For what?'

'The murder of course.'

'Oh, I see.'

Dundee suggested, 'Let's use a process of elimination.'

Eccles said, 'Well, the wife's a possible. Not as meek and mild as she seems. According to Tom Perry anyway.'

'I thought she was rather sweet.'

'You would!'

'What d'you mean by that?'

'You're a sucker for a pretty face. Remember Agnieska.'

This was the good looking young PC, from a family of Polish origin, who had helped them during the sex-trafficking case. Jack had been tempted then, but Agnieska Grabowski had made it clear she had only wanted his help in getting transferred to CID. Now her ambition had been realised anyway, without Jack's help, and he and Leanne seemed to be on an even keel again.

'Yes, but,' Jack went on, 'she isn't tall enough. Jones, that police surgeon, said the murderer had to be at least as tall as the victim.'

'Then what about the boy. He's definitely tall. A bit strange too. Very close to his mum. Perhaps if he thought his dad was playing away...'

'Hmmm...'

Jack went very quiet. He had slipped into that dreamy state again. Had it been the mention of Grabowski? Dawn went on. 'They'll both have to be brought in for proper questioning.'

Jack snapped out of his dream again. 'What d'you mean? "Proper questioning"?'

'Separately. In an interview room, with the recorder on.'

'Oh, I see. Yes, of course.'

The rain stopped just as suddenly as it had begun. Dawn left the wipers on for a while to deal with the last few droplets, but they began to squeak and she turned them off.

'Any other suspects?'

'The guy that Briggs thought he saw?'

'Ah yes, I wonder who that was. Quite an observant man, *Major* Briggs. And obviously infatuated with little Mrs Talbot.'

'Tom Perry?'

'Never! Really nice guy.'

'Now who's being influenced by personal feelings?'

'Then there's the unknown quantities in the other cottage.'

'Yes. We'll have to find them pronto.'

The sun suddenly reappeared. Dawn flicked down the visor.

'Anyway, we need to get back to the station. Get our reports done. I was hoping to go to the match this afternoon.'

At that moment the radio crackled into life. 'All units in the Wem area. Body discovered on Whixall Moss. Report to Old Fenn's Works. Shropshire Wildlife Study Room. Witnesses waiting.'

'Shit, that's us,' cursed Jack, then closed the call.

NINE

When DI Dundee and DS Eccles reached the classroom at the Moss centre they were directed to Lesia as the person in charge. She told them that she was Miss Williams and took them into a little office off the main classroom. Jack could hardly believe that someone so young and pretty could be leading the course. Lesia explained.

'I'm not normally in charge. But the tutor didn't arrive, so I had to take the group onto the Moss. That's when we saw the body.'

'So who usually runs these things?'

'Bernard. Mr Talbot. He's a brilliant tutor. I have no idea where he is. I tried to contact him, but his phone was switched off.'

Jack and Dawn gave each other significant looks. They knew exactly where Mr Talbot was. But they needed to concentrate on that other find first. And they suspected that if this girl knew that her boss had been murdered she would be too upset to give them any information.

'So,' began Jack, 'tell us what happened when you took the group out onto the Moss. How many of them were in the group? Are they all still here?'

'No. One man had to go home. His wife called. She's having a baby. But I have his name and address.'

Eccles said, 'Go on.'

Lesia spoke carefully. She wanted to get it just right.

'There were eighteen in the group. I took them through the wood and showed them the old railway track, just as Mr Talbot would have done. Then we went out onto the Moss. It was very cold and wet and quite dark, even in the morning. I told them all about the Moss. You know...the history, and the unique botany of the area. I've been working with Mr Talbot for a while now, so I know it off by heart. Then it began to rain quite heavily and we started back. But someone pointed out that little pit where the peat had been dug. I'd told them all that no one was allowed to dig the peat any more. When I looked into the pit there was this...the water was very dark...but I could just see that...body.'

The detectives saw the young girl shudder and tears came to her eyes. Jack wanted to hold her tight for comfort. Eccles said, in her usual business-like manner, 'The SOCO team are already down there, examining the corpse. So we'll know more about it quite soon.'

Dundee asked, 'Did any of the others look into the pit?'

'Well some of them may have glanced in, but it began to rain very heavily so we hurried back here. I asked one of them with a mobile to call the police as we walked back. No one touched anything.'

'Right, I think we can let them go,' said Dundee. 'You have all their names and addresses?'

'Yes, in a file on my laptop.'

'OK. But we'd like you to stay, Miss, er...Williams. We have some information for you.'

This was not going to be easy, thought Jack. This girl obviously had a thing for Bernard Talbot, whose body was by now probably lying on the mortuary slab.

Jack had noticed a kettle and a jar of teabags in the tiny office and there was a small fridge in the corner. 'We've had a busy day, Miss Williams. Would it be possible for us to have a cup of tea? While we talk?'

'Oh sure. I'm Lesia by the way.' She filled the kettle and switched it on. Eccles went next door and told the others that they could go home. When she returned there were cups of steaming tea waiting on a tray with some digestive biscuits.

Eccles took a sip of the tea and looked carefully at Lesia as Dundee began.

'I'm afraid, Miss Williams, we have some very bad news. Your boss...Mr Talbot...is dead.'

Dawn saw the glow fade from Lesia's young black cheeks.

'No. There must be some mistake.'

'I'm afraid not. We attended an incident at Mr Talbot's home this morning.'

'Do you know where that is?' asked Eccles.

'Oh yes. I've seen the address on his mail, but I've never been there. I know it's not far from here.'

Lesia's eyes moistened again, as she began to accept the truth of the news.

'Was it a heart attack? I can't believe that. Bernard kept himself very fit.'

'No.' Dundee watched for Lesia's reaction as he said, 'Mr Talbot was attacked. We have reason to believe that he was murdered.'

Lesia's eyes opened wide, her lips parted, and she silently mouthed the word 'Murdered!' There was no way that shock could have been faked, thought Dundee.

'Who? Why?'

Eccles's years in the force had taught her that in certain conditions anyone was capable of anything, but she just could not imagine this girl wielding that hammer – if it was a hammer. But she might still have been involved in some way.

'That's what we are trying to find out,' said Dundee. 'Can you think of anyone who might have had a grudge against Mr Talbot?'

Lesia thought straight away of Darren and gasped, but then she shook her head. It wouldn't be fair to grass him up without any real evidence.

Both the detectives had noticed that slight hesitation before Lesia denied knowing anyone who may have had murderous thoughts.

This girl will need to be interviewed again, thought Eccles, and in a less friendly manner.

Just then Dundee's radio crackled into life. He answered the call.

'DI Dundee here. Go ahead.'

'Sir, Doc Jones has just called from the Moss. He said you won't be needed at that death. There may have been a crime once. But it would have been at least two thousand years ago. Apparently the body has been preserved by the water in the peat. A forensic archaeologist has been sent for. Someone must have had a hell of a shock when they dug that hole.'

TEN

There was no reason for the detectives to remain at Whixall so they decided to drive back to Shrewsbury. Bernard had usually taken Lesia to and from work, but he hadn't arrived that morning and when she had phoned him there was no reply. Luckily one of her colleagues at the wildlife centre was going near there so he gave her a lift. Now the detectives offered to take her back to Shrewsbury. They were sure that she would be given some time off from her job and she may not want to return to the Moss now that Bernard was dead.

As Eccles drove away from the Moss she kept glancing at Lesia in the interior mirror. She was curled up on the back seat, her cheeks wet with tears. It was obvious that she had thought a great deal of Mr Talbot and had now fully accepted that he was dead.

The roads became wider as they approached Shrewsbury so Dawn did not need to concentrate quite so much on her driving. She asked, 'Lesia, how friendly were you with Mr Talbot?'

There was a long silence, then Lesia whispered, 'I think I was in love with him.'

'You knew he was married?'

Lesia sat up and spoke more forcefully. 'He told me his wife didn't love him any more. I know I was stupid but I'd fancied him since he was my teacher in Birmingham. Then it was just a schoolgirl crush. You know how it is.'

Dawn certainly did. She'd had a terrible crush on Miss Jenks, her biology teacher, who was just beginning her teaching career. She was very young and slim with a mane of natural blonde hair, kept in a simple ponytail. Dawn's heart beat like a drum whenever Miss Jenks came near her desk.

'So you were having an affair with Mr Talbot?'

'It hadn't got that far. But he had kissed me.' Lesia sobbed, adding, 'I'm going to miss him so much.'

Eccles thought of that moment of hesitation when Dundee had asked about anyone who might have had a grudge against Bernard. She decided to try again.

'And you're sure you can't think of anyone who hated him badly enough to want to...'

Eccles noticed that Lesia closed her eyes as she muttered, 'No. No one.'

Dundee hadn't spoken a word since he got into the car. When Dawn glanced across at him she thought he might have fallen asleep. What the hell was wrong with him?

Lesia told them she shared a house with a girl in Monkmoor, a suburb just to the south of the town centre, where in fact the police station was located. That friend, Katie, was at home when the detectives accompanied Lesia to the house. Seeing the tears in Lesia's eyes Katie went straight to her and gave her a hug.

'What's wrong, Lees? Why are you home so early?'

Jack explained, 'It's Mr Talbot. He's been killed.'

'What d'you mean? A road accident?'

Suddenly Lesia howled. 'No, Katie. Someone killed him. On purpose.'

'Oh my God!'

Eccles took charge. 'Perhaps we could all sit down. Have a cup of tea.'

'Of course,' said Katie.

'No thanks,' said Lesia, hanging her coat behind the door. 'I'd rather go to bed.'

They could all see that she was trembling, obviously with shock, thought Dawn.

Lesia went to her room and quickly changed into her winter pyjamas. In the bathroom she didn't even bother to clean her teeth. She felt thoroughly disturbed. Bernard dead! How could that be? If she was a drinker perhaps she would have downed a few brandies. Then she remembered the pills the doctor had given her when Darren had started pestering her. He said they'd help her to relax. She took the box from the cabinet, swallowed three pills, then looked at the box and saw that two was the stated dose. Oh well, if they helped...

She lay on her bed and pulled the duvet over her. Now she felt warm and safe and soon drifted off into a deep sleep.

When Dawn went up to check, the girl was fast asleep. She did not disturb her but slipped out of the room and returned downstairs, where she found Katie and Jack in earnest discussion.

'So this guy Darren caused a few problems. Do you know where he lives?'

'Somewhere in Birmingham. That's all I know.'

Eccles sat down and asked, 'What's this all about?'

'Katie has been telling me about a guy called Darren. Apparently he was Lesia's boyfriend when she lived in Birmingham. Black like herself. Bit of a tearaway. Then she chucked him. But he wouldn't accept it. Found out she'd moved to Shrewsbury and began bothering her here.'

'What happened?'

'Well,' said Katie, 'my fiancé, Simon, is training to be a lawyer. He told Darren that if he didn't leave Lesia alone he would get a restraining order. A few days later Simon got beaten up on his way here. He likes to walk everywhere to keep fit. He was coming along the riverside path when he was attacked. It was very dark so Simon couldn't see his attacker properly. Of course we knew who it was. We informed the police about the attack and, thank God, we haven't seen Darren since.'

'Well, well...I think we need to talk to this Darren,' said Dundee. 'What's his surname?'

'I can't remember. You'll have to ask Lesia?'

'Yes, but not now,' said Eccles. 'She needs to sleep. And anyway there'll be a record of that attack on police files. His name will be on that.'

'I don't think it will be. You see Lesia wouldn't accept that Darren was the attacker. She said it could be anybody. So she refused to name him.'

'Damn,' said Jack. 'Well, we'll have to come back in the morning and speak to Miss Williams. We have a press conference to attend this evening at the station. Perhaps you could tell her we'll be coming back tomorrow. What time do you leave for work?'

'About eight fifteen. It's only a short walk.'

Jack rose stiffly from the comfortable armchair.

'Thank you, miss...You've been very helpful.'

Dawn stood too.

'Until tomorrow then. Round about eight.'

When the detectives had gone Katie opened a bottle of wine, put a ready meal in the microwave and sat at the kitchen table, thinking about Mr Talbot and the dreadful thing that had happened. Poor Lesia. She was so upset.

ELEVEN

It was more than a year since Jane had last visited Shropshire. Then she had returned to be with her father, who had suffered a stroke. He was in hospital at Bridgeport, the nearest town to the village where she had lived with her parents until she left for university. Her father had died about a week after his stroke and Jane, with the help of the vicar and the undertakers, had arranged his funeral at the village church.

She'd always had a difficult relationship with her father. When she was a little girl he hardly noticed her. He was too busy writing his crime novels which began to sell quite well, so eventually they could move to a bigger house in the village. Jane had never read any of his books until she was an adult and then she found them repetitive and rather misogynistic. He eventually had an offer from a company to film one of his books and, although the film was never made, the contract made him quite well off.

He hadn't shown much interest in her schooling. But when she was about twelve, and attending the local grammar school, there was a peculiar incident when a school friend, called Moira, came to stay overnight. Jane found out later that her father had sat this girl on his knee to show her his latest manuscript. She was rather well developed for her age and had long fair hair. She had been what you might call a buxom blonde. Jane was out at a music lesson at the time. Her mother had returned home unexpectedly. She was never allowed to have any friends to stay over after that.

In her mid-teens Jane got involved with some bad company and was caught shoplifting. Her father was horrified, but went to the shop and cleared everything up, to save embarrassment to himself.

He was upset when she chose to do science subjects at A level, because he had no understanding of science himself. When she applied to do a science course at university he tried to stop her going, but his wife threatened to tell the world about the incident with the school friend, so he made no further difficulties. It was obvious that her parents no longer loved one another. There weren't many quarrels any more, because they lived quite separate lives. On the other hand, Jane and her mother had been very close until her death four years ago.

During adult life her relationship with her father grew even more distant, but when he had his stroke she had felt it was her duty as his only child to be with him. And it was at his funeral that a young woman's corpse had been discovered in his grave.

Last night she and Patrick had stayed at a hotel in Bridgeport, but they had spent the evening with Jane's old school friend Moira, the girl who had been fondled by her father all those years ago. They had not seen one another since Jane had left school but when she returned to Bridgeport to be with her father they had, by an extraordinary coincidence, met again. Moira had told her about that time with her father. She had rather idolised him as a famous author and felt that he had given her more time and attention than her own parents.

She and Moira had talked about the events at her father's funeral. Jane hadn't been with Patrick then because he'd been unfaithful to her and they had parted, but the investigation into the death of that girl and the subsequent exposure of a sex-trafficking gang had brought them back together. It had been a long time before Patrick had fully earned her trust but now they were truly partners again.

Now his beloved Porsche was making a throaty gurgle as it ate its way along the Shrewsbury bypass. Patrick shouted above the engine noise. 'We're making good time, Jane. Should be there by lunchtime.'

They were heading for a part of Shropshire she hardly knew, so close to the Welsh border that, Patrick had informed her, it had changed hands from English to Welsh and back again several times. This trip was a sort of mini-honeymoon, without a wedding to precede it, as they had both been exceptionally busy for the last few months. They were going to spend a few days in Oswestry. Patrick had researched the place on Google and discovered that its name was derived from 'Oswald's Tree' because King Oswald, who was also a saint, had met his end in a battle there and his body had been left hanging from a tree. There was a gruesome appendage to the tale. Apparently an eagle had removed Oswald's arm and flown away with it. But the arm had dropped from the eagle's talons and where it had landed a spring erupted and had been flowing ever since.

'There are so many places nearby that deserve a visit, Jane. There's a castle at Whittington and another at Chirk. There are Meres at Ellesmere and a place called Whixall Moss.'

Jane wondered what that was, but Patrick was in full flight.

'There are canals and aqueducts, especially the famous one at Pontcysyllte, which is a World Heritage Site...'

The problem with all this for Jane was that it was only February and she wasn't sure she wanted to be traipsing about as a tourist in the cold and wet. Their reunion had been recent enough for her to be happy spending most of the time in bed with Patrick.

In fact she was feeling quite sleepy now. Jane had drunk rather too much of Moira's splendid wine last night. Patrick had managed to be unusually abstemious because he would be driving his precious Porsche again, next day, but he'd still been good company.

Patrick was quite well off because he owned a technology company. It was his skill with clever gadgets that had enabled their good friends DI Dundee and DS Eccles to track down the location of that sex-trafficking gang and bring them to justice. They'd been helped in this adventure by a very brave and beautiful young policewoman called Agnieska Grabowski and also by poor young Pete Staines.

Jane would have loved to meet Dundee and Eccles again while they were in Bridgeport but apparently they'd been transferred to another district and Moira wasn't sure where they'd gone and as this was only going to be short break there wasn't really time to make enquiries. And she wasn't quite sure she trusted Patrick well enough yet for a reunion with the stunning Grabowski.

They dumped their cases in the hotel room and went out to stretch their legs. The weather was still cold and the low clouds threatened rain, but they were well wrapped up and ready to explore.

Opposite the hotel there was a large church. They went over to examine it. The tower was obviously very old and surrounded by ancient yew trees whose trunks were like the gnarled veins on the back of an old man's hand. Among these trees there was also an old lamp post, probably a gas lamp originally, which reminded Jane of the one in *The Lion, the Witch and the Wardrobe*. Most of the gravestones had been piled up to make a sort of wall around the graveyard and many of those left were leaning precariously or had actually tumbled over.

They hadn't stopped yesterday to visit her parents' graves. Her father had requested to be buried beside his wife. She didn't really know why, because they hadn't shared much in life for many years. Patrick had promised that they would visit the graves on their return journey. A few months ago Jane had telephoned a funeral director in Bridgeport and asked them to erect a simple stone with his name and dates on her father's grave. She had not seen the stone yet. She wondered why she'd bothered. He was a strange, unlikeable man who had begun the events that led to the death of the young woman who had been found in his grave. He wasn't directly responsible for her death but even so...and when I've gone, she thought, those graves will be as neglected as the ones in this churchyard.

She looked up to see Patrick reading another stone.

'Another "in loving memory",' he said. 'But who remembers them now?'

She smiled. 'What morbid thoughts! Come on let's get out of here.'

At that moment the clock in the old tower began to sound the hour of two. For some reason it made her think of her friend Tony, who had been so helpful during that dreadful time last winter. He always said , 'No regrets, Jane.' It was Tony who'd advised her to get back together with Patrick before it was too late.

As the bell tolled on she thought about Tony's advice, 'The clock's ticking, Jane. Surely you want kids?'

Did she want children? After all she was nearly forty years old. Since their reunion she hadn't bothered to take the pill. It was unlikely that she would get pregnant and when she told Patrick he didn't seem to mind. So they had shared a good deal of wonderful, unprotected sex. For the last couple of days she had felt rather different in the mornings, with slight nausea and tender breasts, but that was probably just her period approaching. Patrick was a few years older than her. She wondered how he would he feel about becoming a father.

They came out of the churchyard onto a road called Welsh Walls. On their way into the town Patrick had pointed out a street called English Walls. Now he exclaimed, 'This certainly is a border town.'

They walked towards the centre of the town, which was busy on this market day. There were all the usual shops, and the usual proliferating charity shops and a few abandoned ones, as there were everywhere these days. The market was quite lively, even on this dull day. There was an indoor market and a few stalls outside in a square surrounded by pubs and a rather fine building which was apparently the council offices. They climbed the castle mound and saw the town spread beneath them. It really was quite a small place. On one side the landscape towards the east was mainly flat while on the western side it rose to a range of tree covered hills.

The rain began again and they hurried back to the hotel. Back in their room, as they were getting out of their wet clothes, Patrick turned on the television just as the local news began. The main item was about a nasty murder which had happened that morning at a place near Whixall, which rang a bell.

'Wasn't Whixall one of the places you mentioned this morning, Patrick.'

'That's right,' he said. 'It's not far from here.'

She pointed at the screen. 'Oh look!' A tall, handsome middle aged man in a dark suit was addressing a posse of reporters. 'It's Jack Dundee!'

'And there's Dawn,' said Patrick.

'So where are they now?'

'I think the reporter mentioned Shrewsbury police station.'

They'd switched on the set too late to catch the details and before they could really understand what had happened the newsreader moved on to another item. But they decided then that they must try and contact Jack and Dawn the next day.

TWELVE

In her nightmare Lesia was walking across the Moss with Bernard when he suddenly collapsed. She thought he must have had a heart attack and tried to revive him, but then she saw that blood was pouring from his head. She left him and ran off to get help, sliding on the wet turf and slipping into the water at the side of the track. Then the scene faded.

She slowly returned to consciousness, still wondering where she was and what was going on. There was someone standing over her bed, a vague shape in the darkened room. She started to scream but a strong hand clamped over her mouth and nothing came out. Then the hand was replaced by some thick material which made it impossible to do more than whimper. Her head was lifted and the material, which she guessed must be a scarf, was tied at the back. She tried to kick and scratch her attacker but he sprawled across the duvet trapping her arms and legs underneath. Her attacker rolled her in the duvet as if it was a carpet and carried her downstairs. She was still partly under the influence of those pills and felt herself slipping back into unconsciousness, and wondered if she was still dreaming.

In the living room the man laid her on the settee and wrapped a belt around the duvet so that she was swaddled like a native-American papoose. She tried to call Katie but it was impossible to make any real sound. In the half-light she saw her attacker go to the front door, open it and look around. Then he returned and she realised he was wearing a mask. Now she was terrified. A man who wore a mask intended to do evil. She wriggled as much as she could but to no avail.

Her abductor lifted her and carried her outside. He was obviously very strong. At this early hour of the morning there was no one about. The air was very cold, almost frosty. He opened the rear door of a car, manoeuvred her inside and laid her on the back seat. At least he had made sure that she did not bang her head. Lesia stirred, wriggled again, and tried to shake off the scarf but it was firmly fixed. Her attacker quietly closed the car door, and disappeared for a moment. She did not see him, but he went back to the house and carefully closed that door, then looked around. There was no sign of life inside and no lights had been turned on.

He had been surprised that Lesia had not put up more of a fight. He did not know that she had been partially sedated. He smiled and muttered, 'Brilliant, man!'

He got into the driving seat. The heater had been on full blast while he drove here, so even though the rear door had been opened briefly the car was still pleasantly warm inside. He had had the sense to 'borrow' a fairly new car so the engine caught first time and purred gently as he accelerated slowly away, then he upped his speed as he drove out of the town, heading north.

After driving for about forty minutes on main roads he turned down a narrow country lane and came to a canal. Again he smiled to himself. This was the perfect place. There was this little offshoot from the main canal, perhaps they were going to build another canal but had only managed a couple of hundred yards before giving up. There were no houses nearby. Leafless trees hung over the water from both sides creating a dark tunnel, so that the boats moored there were almost hidden. The towpath here was quite neglected, because the proper towpath went over a nearby bridge and continued along the other side of the canal.

There were three narrowboats moored at this quiet spot. Two of them closed up for the winter. The other apparently shut up as well, but in fact there was smoke rising from the chimney and slivers of light showed through the slight gaps around the shutters.

The young man stepped onto the boat and opened the door in the stern. Then he returned to the car, carefully lifted Lesia out, carried her to the boat and down a few steps into the main cabin. He laid her on one of the long seats that could be converted to beds. He checked that the scarf was still acting as a gag. He really hated doing this and he doubted whether her screams would be heard even if she managed to remove the scarf, which would be difficult because her arms were still encased in the duvet. But it would only be for a short time and he had to be sure.

He locked the door, left the boat and drove the car a mile or so down the main road, where he returned it to the driveway of a large house set among trees. He had found the keys carelessly left in the car when he saw it on the driveway. How stupid was that. Now he parked the car behind two others, just out of range of the security light, then carefully wiped the steering wheel and the lever for the automatic gears to remove any fingerprints. He locked the car door, wiped the ignition key, dropped it into an envelope on which he had written 'Found on the road' and pushed it through the letter box with his gloved hand. Of course the security light came on but he reckoned that the people in the house were all fast asleep at this hour of the morning, and that they would be so pleased to have the keys returned safely that they wouldn't bother about the light coming on, probably thinking it was a fox. The light soon went off as the young man ran into the trees which surrounded the house, stepped through onto the canal towpath and jogged back to the place where the boat was moored.

When he entered the cabin he saw Lesia's eyes staring at him, wide open with terror and heard her muttering something. He locked the door of the cabin, took off the mask he had been wearing, undid the belt around the duvet and finally removed the scarf from around her mouth. Lesia was still woozy but she burst out, 'Darren! What the fucking hell...!'

'Lesia, please listen to me. I'm not going to hurt you. I just need to talk to you. That restraining order meant I couldn't come and talk to you like I wanted. So I had to do it this way.'

'You're a fool. You'll go to prison for this.'

Lesia tried to stand up but found that her legs wouldn't obey her. She began to cry. Darren went over to sit beside her but she drew away.

'Don't you touch me or I'll scream.'

'You won't be heard. We're miles from anywhere. Please just listen to me. In the morning I'll call a taxi to take you home.'

Darren's voice was so calm and his eyes so full of pleading that Lesia relaxed a little. If he had intended to hurt her he would have done so already.

There was a stove in the cabin so it was quite warm. Lesia was only dressed in her pyjamas, so she hugged the duvet around her. Darren went to the stove, lifted a kettle and poured some boiling water into a cup. He added some coffee from a jar and stirred it round. He handed the cup to Lesia. She took a sip and smiled. She knew now that Darren intended her no harm.

'OK. Go ahead. What d'you want to tell me?'

Darren took a deep breath.

'First, I love you. I have loved you since we first met.'

'This is a bloody funny way of showing it.'

'I realise now that I wanted to take things further than you wanted to go. I was stupid. I should have waited till you were ready. I'm really sorry.'

Lesia nodded to accept his apology.

'Then that other guy came along. Bernard. That white guy with his posh talk and fancy car. I didn't stand a chance. But...'

Lesia burst into tears and whispered, 'Bernard is dead.'

Darren was truly shocked. 'Dead?'

'He was murdered.'

'Christ!'

'I even thought you might have done it. Out of jealousy.'

'Oh, come on, Lesia. I may bend the law from time to time. But murder!'

'No, I suppose not.'

'And that's the other thing I wanted to tell you. Bernard is... was...not what you thought he was. I did some digging. He was a crook.'

'Rubbish!'

'No. It's true. He was involved with some really nasty types. That's probably why he took the job out in that godforsaken place. He was using it for his real business. Drugs!'

'That's nonsense. Bernard loved the Moss. He knew everything about it. He was a brilliant teacher.'

'It was a very clever cover. For his real business.'

'I don't believe a word of this. I loved him. He loved me.'

'Of course he did. You're a lovely young woman. He wanted to get you into his bed.'

'Like you!' Lesia snapped.

'Yes, I admit it. Now I know I was wrong. Perhaps if I'd waited. One day...'

'Never. Bernard was going to leave his wife. Get a divorce.'

'Yeah, I'm sure.'

'OK, what makes you think he was a crook?'

'Right. First there's that car of his. How much d'you think they cost new?'

'No idea. But it was a nice car. Very comfortable.'

'It should be for more than forty grand.'

'What?'

'So how does a teacher afford that?'

Lesia couldn't answer for a moment, then she said, 'He inherited it. Or won the lottery.'

'Perhaps. But look at these.'

He took out a phone. Not his usual phone. This one had a special purpose.

'You see. He used to take you home, then go back to that place. I followed him one night. On that mate's motorbike. The guy drove right down onto the...what d'they call it...the Moss...no problem in a car like that. I hid the bike and followed him. There was another car down there among the trees. The driver got out. He had a big torch. I took this.'

He showed Lesia the screen of the phone. There was Bernard handing over a small packet to the man.

'And this.'

In the next picture the guy was handing Bernard what looked like a wad of cash.

'Then they got in their cars and drove away. The same thing happened the next night and the next.'

Lesia was stunned. It was obvious that something illegal was going on. Otherwise why meet in that lonely spot after dark. She racked her brain to find an excuse for Bernard, but nothing came.

'So why was he murdered?'

'Something went wrong. Thieves always fall out in the end.'

'What d'you think was in those packets?'

'I know exactly what it was.'

He lifted the cushion off the other bench, removed the wooden base and brought out a small package wrapped in plastic. He took out a penknife and was about to cut into the packet, when a figure appeared in the doorway and a deep voice spoke, 'Put that down and stick your hands in the air. Now!'

DAY TWO

THIRTEEN

When Dundee reached the station early next morning he went straight to his office for coffee and a few moments of quiet contemplation before the morning briefing. He hardly ever read a newspaper, preferring to catch up with the news on Radio Shropshire, partly because he never had time to read a paper properly and because so much of what was in them was a sheer waste of time. Sometimes he would glance at the back page of *The Shropshire Star* for news of the local football team, but this morning someone had left a copy of one of the dailies on his desk with a small article on page 2 ringed round in pencil. Jack picked up the pencil and underlined the misspellings and inaccuracies in the report.

'Murder on the Moss

Our crime reporter Mark Witterword attended a press conference last night at Shrewsbury police station. Here is his report.

Police incompetence

In the early hours of yesterday morning the body of Mr Bernard Tablet was found in his own home in a quiet backwater near Shrewsbury. We are used to violence on the streets of London, Birmingham or Manchester, but for a brutal murder to take place in such a quiet, rural spot is very shocking. Of course police resources are limited these days but the north Shropshire force is not exactly overworked. The two detectives investigating the murder found fame locally a couple of years ago in a child sex case. But this time they haven't a clue, in spite of the fact that the dead man had obviously been killed by a blow to the front of the head and there was blood everywhere.

The dead man, Mr Brian Talbot, was employed by the Shropshire Wildlife Company as a warden at Whixall Moss, the famous peat bog. His home, Willow Cottage, is close to the

Moss. He is survived by his wife, Julie, a pretty blonde in her late forties and his son Paul, aged 17. They are both helping the police with their enquiries. A neighbour, Mr Roland Biggins, heard the wife screaming and went to investigate. He telephoned the police but it took them several hours to arrive on the scene. Biggins said he thought he had seen someone running away from the cottage but couldn't be sure. Scene of Crime officers have scoured the area but have come up with absolutely nothing so far.

Afterwards I had an exclusive interview with DC Beccles, who told me that they were pursuing a wide range of enquiries in the area and hoped to find the culprit before too long. Let us hope she is right. For such a violent act to take place in such a peaceful spot makes us all worry about our safety.'

Dundee sighed. How could they print such rubbish? Was the subeditor dyslexic? Did they never try to verify the facts? Why were they always so keen to denigrate the police? But at least he had escaped from that journalist in south Shropshire who had a vendetta against him. After an early altercation a reporter called Dan Mathews had tried constantly to smear Dundee's reputation. But Mathews had published an article that had led indirectly to the death of a witness, and had been sent back to reporting WI meetings and local flower shows by the local rag.

Dundee chucked the newspaper in the bin, quickly checked his appearance reflected in the glass door, opened it and walked off to the ops room, where his colleagues would be waiting.

FOURTEEN

There were two of them. One was middle aged, tall and broad, with one of the ugliest faces Lesia had ever seen. He looked as if he'd spent his life getting knocked about in a boxing ring. The other one was young, short and podgy, with the face of a schoolboy and a stupid grin. The older one calmly picked up Darren's knife and pocketed it; in his other hand he held a gun, which at that moment was pointed at Darren.

'So what the hell are you two niggers doing on this boat,' he said.

Lesia gasped. It was a long time since she'd heard someone use that horrid word. She had known at once that these were not just boatmen. They were dangerous and racist to boot.

She glanced at Darren and saw fear flicker in his eyes. But when he spoke he tried to sound cool.

'Look, I'm sorry, mate. I didn't think anyone was using the boat. I just wanted somewhere quiet to snog my girl. That right, Lesia?'

She nodded. The older man smiled, with a nasty curl of the lips.

'Then you found the gear and decided to get a fix.'

'What fix? What gear?'

'Oh, come on,' said the man with the gun. 'You blacks are tripping all the time.'

The man's lips had curled further and he lifted the gun towards Darren's head. The younger one was nodding like an idiot. Lesia was really frightened by him.

'OK,' said Darren. 'So I knew what this was. But my girl ain't into that sort of stuff. Please let her go.'

'And have her run straight to the filth. You must be joking.'

Lesia forced herself to speak at last; her voice cracking with fear.

'So what you going to do with us?'

The man narrowed his eyes and studied her.

'Well, my pretty little nigger. Perhaps I should let Piggy have some fun with you.'

The younger man licked his lips and seemed to shiver with anticipation.

'But I don't think your boyfriend would like that very much.'

Darren stiffened. Lesia thought he might try something stupid. She shook her head, hoping he would understand. The man went on.

'But we don't have time. We've got to move out. See, that stupid bastard getting killed has made it too hot round here. So we're moving the operation. And when that's done we might be able to let you go.'

For the first time since these men had arrived Lesia thought that they might be going to come out of this alive, then her hopes were dashed when he handed the gun to the younger man.

'Right, Piggy, I'm going back to the car for a few things. Keep an eye on our friends. If they try anything stupid you know what to do.'

Lesia began sweat and shiver at the same time. The big man went on.

'You see,' he said, 'Piggy ain't got much up top, but he's a crack shot when he needs to be.'

Piggy's grin grew wider and he nodded vigorously. The man picked up the package and left the boat.

Piggy pointed the gun first at Darren, then at Lesia and chuckled to himself. He slowly approached Lesia, put out a hand towards her left breast and stroked the nipple. She saw his trousers bulge between his legs and wanted to kick him hard in that very spot. She heard Darren give a moan of frustration and willed him not to try anything. She wondered how far Piggy would go before Darren lost his rag.

Suddenly Piggy moved away from Lesia and pointed the gun at Darren instead. He muttered, 'Black bastard. Black bastard,' several times in a moronic chant. Lesia looked around for something to use as a weapon. If she didn't do something soon Darren would try to attack him and get shot at close range. Then she had an idea. She spoke to Piggy in the voice of a vamp and began to unbutton the top of her pyjamas.

'I like you, Piggy. I bet you know what a girl needs.'

If she could just distract him for a moment Darren might be able to...

But at that moment the big man returned. He had a coil of rope over his shoulder, and a couple of bottles of what looked like spring water in his hand.

'OK, Piggy. Move back a bit. Keep the gun on the guy while I deal with the girl. Right you two. You can relax. I've decided to let you live.'

He moved over to Lesia, who winced as she smelt his breath. He tied her wrists together. She realised she could still move her fingers, which might be useful.

'I'm going to tie you up and leave you on the boat till we've moved on. Then I'll let the pigs know you're here.'

He pushed her back onto the seat, lifted her legs and began to tie them together as well. Finally he leant over her as if he was going to give her a kiss. She wanted to throw up. She thought he was going to put something over her mouth but instead he put the bottle of water near her.

'You see, I'm really a nice guy. I don't want you to die of thirst. Don't try to drink the water on the boat. It has to be boiled first. And I'm going to put out the stove, so no one sees smoke coming out of the chimney. I don't need to gag you 'cause this is the most lonely spot on the whole canal. You can shout as much as you like.' He checked his watch.' There won't be no one round here at three in the morning.'

He moved over to Darren with another piece of rope. Darren tried to resist. The big man punched him on the head and he passed out.

'That's better,' the man muttered. 'Bit of peace and quiet.'

He swiftly tied Darren's wrists and ankles and sat him on the floor. Lesia was relieved when she saw that he was slowly coming round again.

'Now, boys and girls, I'm going to turn off the generator so the lights will go off in a while but I don't reckon you'll have to spend more than few hours here. That's if everything goes as planned. And at least you've got each other for company.'

The man put another bottle of water near Darren. He laughed and said, 'Be good.' Then he turned to Piggy. 'You can put the gun away. They won't be causing any problems now.'

Both men went up the steps to the deck and locked the solid door. Lesia heard a car pull away, then total silence fell.

FIFTEEN

It was just after eight next morning when DS Eccles rang the bell of the small house in Monkmoor which Katie shared with Lesia. When Katie opened the door it was obvious that something was wrong.

'What is it?' asked Dawn.

'I just went up to tell Lesia you were coming to talk to her. But she wasn't there. I've looked all over the house. She's disappeared.'

'You didn't hear anything in the night?'

'No, I was dead to the world. Too much vino. Simon couldn't come round last night, so I was on my own. I kept thinking about that dreadful murder. By the time I finally got to sleep we could have been burgled and I wouldn't have heard a thing.'

'Has she taken anything with her?'

'No, that's what's so odd. Her coat's still behind the door and nothing seems to be missing from her wardrobe.'

'Do you mind if we take a look?' asked DI Dundee.

'No. Go ahead. I have to go to work anyway. Please lock up when you leave. There's a spare key in the kitchen. Just drop it through the letter box. And keep me informed. I'm really worried about Lesia. I mean why would she disappear like that in the middle of the night? I work at Harley and Sons, the estate agents. We're really busy at the moment. I daren't miss a day.'

'We'll ring you.'

Dundee and Eccles went up to Lesia's room. It was all neat and tidy. There was an empty suitcase on top of the wardrobe and inside the wardrobe a row of clothes filled it from side to side. But the duvet that Dawn had spread over Lesia last night had disappeared.

'You know,' said Dawn. 'It's almost as if Lesia had been lifted from that bed and carried away.'

'Hmm...' muttered Jack. 'I think we should see if we can find some reference to that guy, Darren. A diary or a letter perhaps.'

'We don't really have the right to look at her things.'

'Oh, come on, Dawn. The kid's missing. Taken none of her things. It's pretty obvious she hasn't left of her own accord. We need to find her quick.'

But there was no diary. There was a row of books on a small bookcase, mainly about natural history, interspersed with a few modern novels. There was a notebook on the bedside table, filled with neat sketches of plants.

This information brought another muttered 'Hmm...' from DI Dundee. The only letters were from Lesia's parents and there a short note from Bernard telling Lesia how fond of her he was.

There was a sturdy chest of drawers and a matching dressing table both from an earlier era. The detectives checked the drawers in both, but found nothing except neatly folded clothes and some basic make-up.

'That's it then,' said Dawn. 'No sign of our friend Darren.'

'Tell you what's strange, Dawn. Have you seen a phone? All kids have a smartphone these days. So where's hers?'

'Good point, Jack. So whoever took Lesia, and I reckon she was taken, made sure they took her phone as well.'

Just at that moment a phone sounded somewhere downstairs. Jack hurried down, as fast as his bulk would allow, and followed the sound to a coat hanging up behind the door. He felt through the pockets until he pulled out a phone but at that moment the caller rang off.

'Damn!' exclaimed Jack. He passed the phone to Dawn. 'D'you reckon this is her phone?'

'I'd put money on it. She left her coat down here last night and was too tired to check her phone.'

Dawn quickly scrolled down the phone's screen, then smiled. 'Well, well. Look at that, Jack.'

DI Dundee peered at the screen, holding the phone at arm's length. He must arrange an eye test soon.

There in the list of contacts was the name Darren and the number beside it. Dawn called the number but it soon went to voicemail.

'Right, we must get that phone back to the station.'

The techies would soon find the location of Darren's phone and then they'd catch its owner.

Just as they were about to leave the house a call came through on Jack's phone from Davies the crime scene manager.

'Hi, Jack. I'm back at Lilac Cottage. We've just found a bloodstained jacket hidden under a bush on the Moss, just behind that little copse. It's a parka type coat with a camouflage pattern. I just hope all the rain hasn't washed away any DNA.'

They hurried to the station ready to search for Darren, but when Dundee reached his office he found a note on his desk asking him to phone the study centre at the Moss and speak to DC Perkins. Jack lifted the phone on his desk and rang the number. Perkins must have been waiting for him to call because he answered straight away and his voice sounded excited.

'Hi there. Derek Perkins speaking.'

'This is DI Dundee. You wanted me to call?'

'Yes, Jack.'

'Well?'

'It's about that body found on the Moss.'

'I thought that was a couple of thousand years old. No concern of ours.'

'Yes, Jack, that's right. But I'm not calling about the body itself. Something else was found in the same hole when they removed the corpse.'

'Go on.'

'A leather bag. Almost new.'

'Strange...'

'Not as strange as what was found in the bag.'

'Which was?'

'Bank notes, Jack. Several thousand pounds worth. Mainly in new fifties.'

'Bloody hell! So where's this bag now?'

'Here, waiting for you to check it out.'

SIXTEEN

Paul had to get out of the house for a while. All those policemen still bumbling about in their muddy boots. And the way they kept looking at him.

Of course his mum was very upset. He knew she'd stopped loving Dad, probably even hated him, especially since he began to hit her, but for such a dreadful thing to happen right here in their own house. Horrible!

He'd just walk for a while across the Moss. Be on his own and think about things. He knew it was a mistake coming to live out here. He'd been happy in Birmingham. He loved the busy streets and the real mix of people. And the way you were accepted for what you were. Out here they are all white and straight and stupid. And in this place there was absolutely nothing interesting to do. Paul used to go to the City Art Gallery at least once a week. All those wonderful pre-Raphaelite paintings and tapestries. And the cinema. He and Mum went to see all the latest films. Here, there was just trees and sky and that dreadful Moss. If you didn't know what you were doing it was so easy to miss the path and sink into the swamp.

At least the weather was a bit better today. It was still cold but the sun was shining. Oh look, there was one of those nasty birds, buzzards, that's what Dad called them. It was hovering just above him. They swoop down on small creatures and tear them apart. He had seen them sitting on a fence post at the end of the garden. And if he tried to frighten them they simply dropped their prey and flew off.

Paul even used to like his school in Birmingham. Had some good friends. They'd been together since primary. He hated the school he went to now. All those thickoes and bullies. And the teachers were pathetic. Except David of course. He taught art. He knew at once that Paul was talented. The others just knew he was different. He tried to tell Dad about the bullies, but all he said was, 'Stand up for yourself, boy. They're all cowards really.' Just because he used to do a bit of boxing. OK, so Paul was tall for his age and could probably hurt one of them, but there was never just one.

His dad never really liked him. Well, not since he was a little kid. All those awful walks in the country, mile after mile, and all that talk about this plant and that animal, and Mum saying her feet hurt and could we go home.

Paul had wanted to come out for some time. But he knew Dad would go berserk. Sorry! Would have gone berserk. He must remember that Dad was dead. Perhaps now...Mum had known what he was for some time. She didn't care. She just loved him. He knew that she hated it out here too. If it wasn't for David, she would probably have left a while ago. She hasn't made any other friends. She never has a chance to dress up now. And she's so pretty, when she wears one of her dresses and has her hair done. Paul remembered when she went to the parents' evening. All those idiots in his class staring at her and making obscene remarks. Of course that was when she had met David.

Time to go back. Or they might think he'd run off. He knew there was one of the coppers who really thought he'd done it. Watched his every move. And when they found that coat that clinched it so far as he was concerned. As if Paul would wear a bloody coat like that. Christ, what a tasteless pun. He would never wear anything that suggested the army. But when they tested that coat they wouldn't find any evidence of him. There wasn't much blood on the floor from that wound. It must all have gone on that coat. So the person who was wearing that coat must have been the murderer. Then he must have carried Dad's body to the house and dumped him in the hallway. Perhaps there were two of them. Dad's body would have been quite heavy.

When Mum had seen Dad's body she had gone so white that Paul thought she'd be sick. Then she screamed and screamed. Until Briggs came. At last Paul had managed to calm her down. He loved her very much. He'd do anything for her. Anything at all.

SEVENTEEN

The detectives' day continued to be very frustrating. Of course the techies were soon able to locate Darren's phone. They gave Dundee and Eccles an address on the other side of town so they drove over the English Bridge, up the steep hill called Wyle Cop and into the one way system through the town centre. The traffic became heavy and as they crawled along the High Street Jack went into daydream mode again.

Dawn tried to ask Jack what was bothering him, but he didn't seem to hear her, so she drove on in silence except for the occasional crackle from the radio. They reached the Welsh Bridge and crossed into Frankwell, an ancient part of the town, which they had heard used to be under water most winters until the flood barriers were built. Since then Frankwell had become quite trendy, with the new theatre and a number of cafés, and it had lost some of its reputation for being a red light district. They parked in the Riverside Car Park and walked to the flats where they met the landlord as arranged. He told them that Darren had suddenly left the flat a couple of days ago, owing a month's rent. But when the landlord let them into the tiny flat, more of a bedsit really, they found everything neat and tidy as if Darren intended to return. There were a few clothes in a wardrobe and chest of drawers on which stood a photograph of Lesia obviously taken a few years ago. There was a copy of *The Shropshire Star* lying folded on a table but when Dundee studied it, with gloved hands, he saw it was yesterday's edition and had hardly been opened, so Darren had been here yesterday and it looked as if he had left in a hurry. It was more obvious than ever that they needed to find him soon because he might have been involved in or have some news of the missing girl.

Back at the station Jack found a message on his desk to phone a number he didn't immediately recognise. When he rang it he was surprised and pleased to hear a familiar voice. It was ages since they'd last met, at Pete's funeral. Jane explained that she was visiting Shropshire with Patrick on a brief holiday and would love to meet up with him and Dawn, if that was possible. Dundee explained that they were in the middle of a case but that he would phone back later that day, when he had spoken to Dawn, and that it might be possible to arrange something for that evening.

Jack told Dawn about the call while they drove round to Katie's house, just in case Lesia had returned, but no one answered the door when they rang the bell, so they drove north-westwards out of the town towards Whixall where the bag and all that cash lay waiting.

It was the size of a large handbag. The brown leather was completely saturated but once it had dried out it could be taken round the shops in Shrewsbury which sold that kind of bag just in case they had a record of the sale. The trouble is that so much these days is bought on the internet, but someone at the station could check through the various outlets, try to identify the style of the bag and make enquiries.

The money was wrapped in clear plastic and had remained dry. When the exact amount had been counted and the denominations recorded the local banks could be contacted in case they had a record of such a withdrawal. Trouble was, the money could have been withdrawn from any bank anywhere.

Dundee and Eccles took the opportunity to walk across the Moss and inspect the place where the ancient corpse and the modern bag had been found, but there's not much you can learn from a hole in the ground half full of almost black water. The Moss looked unthreatening on this sunny morning, and Dundee thought he would like to bring Leanne and the twins out here for a walk when the weather was warmer. But it might not be just

Leanne and the twins. That was the problem which had been distracting him for a while.

Dawn was intrigued by the idea of that ancient corpse being preserved so well that it had been briefly mistaken for a recent death. She had read a book about other corpses found in the peat bogs in Ireland and Denmark and the evidence they often showed of violent death many centuries ago.

The bag and its contents were wrapped in plastic and the detectives returned to the station and handed them over to forensics, though there wasn't much chance of any fingerprints left on the bag after such a soaking. And there was still no sighting of either Lesia or Darren.

The pathologist's initial report on Bernard Talbot came through. It confirmed that his death had been caused by a blow to the back of the head from a metal object, making a narrow but deep incision into the brain. The pathologist suggested that the weapon might be a small hammer. The rest of the body showed considerable athleticism and there was no evidence of any toxins in the system; in other words a healthy man had been killed by a single blow.

Lesia's parents had been informed of their daughter's disappearance and were waiting at the station when Dundee and Eccles returned. They were distraught and had dropped everything to come to Shrewsbury to do anything they could to help the search. They had no idea where Darren lived. Their daughter had never spoken of him. They knew that Lesia had gone through a brief wild phase – they called it letting off steam – in her late teens but that had soon passed. They knew that she was enjoying her work at the wild life centre and were horrified to learn that her boss, whom Lesia had mentioned a few times, had been murdered.

The parents had brought a recent photograph of Lesia with them. Eccles smiled when she saw such a resemblance between mother and daughter. Mrs Williams was still an attractive woman, though she was slightly heavier than her daughter now and her hair was tinged with grey. The photograph of Lesia would be circulated to the press and shown on the local evening news.

Dundee was impressed with the couple and assured them that everything would be done to find their beloved daughter. Meeting them made him remember his own father who had died of fags and disappointment at a relatively early age and his mother with whom he no longer had any contact. He was thankful that his father had introduced him to the river at Bridgeport, where they had spent many happy weekends fishing from its banks and where he later moved to live and work. He still rather missed Bridgeport but Shrewsbury was also an attractive town with that same river practically encircling it.

EIGHTEEN

Dawn led Julie Talbot into the interview room. It had been difficult to separate her from Paul but at last he had agreed to follow PC Perkins, a good looking young recruit, on a tour of the station. Julie herself was dressed in smart jeans and a clinging sweater, which made her look younger than ever. She was perhaps slightly red around the eyes, but Dawn could not see much else of the grieving widow about her, but perhaps, thought Dawn, that's just my own nasty suspicious mind. She was also concerned about Jack's attitude to their interviewee. He did have such a weakness for attractive women. But there was no sign that he was being taken in by this one as he began the routine.

'Sit down, Mrs Talbot. Thank you for attending this interview.'

Mrs Talbot remained standing and said, 'Did I have a choice? Am I under arrest?'

Dawn broke in.

'No. This is purely routine. Please sit down, Mrs Talbot.'

At last she did so. Jack switched on the recording machine and checked his watch.

'The time is eleven fifteen on the twenty-second of February. This is DI Dundee accompanied by DS Eccles interviewing Mrs Talbot about her husband's murder yesterday.'

Mrs Talbot gave a quick sob and lifted a tissue from the box on the table and wiped her eyes.

'Mrs Talbot, I know that we spoke briefly about what happened yesterday morning, and that you have given us a written statement, but for the purposes of the investigation, can you tell us again exactly what you remember.'

'Well,' Mrs Talbot began. 'When I woke up I was feeling quite woozy. I've been taking sleeping tablets recently because I haven't been sleeping well...'

Dawn asked, 'Why is that?'

'To be perfectly honest, Bernard and I had not been getting on very well. Ever since he dragged us out to that dreadful place. He seemed to spend longer and longer out on the Moss. He thought more of it than he did of me. I mean it's all very well being interested in the natural world, but when it takes over your whole life...And I knew that our constant squabbling had begun to affect Paul. And with GCSEs coming up...'

'How did your husband get on with his son?'

'They've never been that close. Bernard was always outgoing. Very physical. With strong views about everything.'

'Such as?' asked Dawn.

'Oh, conservation, recycling, climate change. All that sort of thing.'

'Whereas Paul?'

'Sensitive, artistic, happiest among creative people.'

'So they didn't really hit it off?'

'No?'

Dundee asked, 'Did he hate his father?'

'I wouldn't say that. Certainly not enough to murder him, if that's what you mean. But Paul loves me very much. And when Bernard started to hit me...'

'When did that happen?'

'A couple of months ago. He thought I was having an affair. With one of the teachers at Paul's school.'

'Were you?'

'Of course not. I like David and we have a great deal in common, but I wouldn't...'

'We shall need to speak to this David. What's his surname?'

'No. That isn't fair. He has nothing to do with what has happened. Why should he be involved?'

'Don't worry,' said Dawn. 'We'll be very discreet. But this is a murder case and we need to speak to everyone who may have information.'

'But he doesn't have any information. I don't think he and Bernard ever met. And he's a married man. I wouldn't want his wife to be upset.'

'Oh, I see. He's a married man,' said Dawn, in a rather judgemental tone. 'I'm sorry, Mrs Talbot, but we will need to talk to him. His wife won't need to know. So what is his name?'

Julie chewed her lip and looked like a schoolgirl caught smoking.

'Very well. His name is Hurst. David Hurst. He teaches Art. Paul enjoys his lessons. My son is quite a talented artist. That's another reason he and Bernard don't get on. Bernard has...' She lifted another tissue from the box and wiped her eyes. '...had no interest in the arts.'

There was a pause in the interview. Julie fluttered her eyelashes at Dundee, but he seemed determined not to be affected. He asked, 'When you say your husband hit you, was he really violent?'

'He slapped my face. It really stung. And he bit my neck. Not in a loving way. And punched my chest. It's still bruised. Look.'

She began to lift her sweater.

'Wait,' said Dawn. 'We'll ask the doctor to examine you. And make a report.'

Julie Talbot pulled her sweater down again but she had already revealed the pale skin of a shapely midriff and the bottom of a black bra. Dundee blushed. Then he became business-like again.

'Right, let's return to yesterday morning. You woke feeling woozy from those tablets. What next?'

'I heard this thump. Like a piece of furniture falling over. Then a click, like the back door being unbolted. I just thought that was Bernard going outside. I told you before. He often gets...got up early and went outside. I was asleep before he came in last night. If he did come in. Alive I mean.'

She paused, as if considering the implications.

'Then?' asked Dundee.

'Do I have to go over all this again?'

'Do you want your husband's murderer to be found? If so, the timing of these events is crucial.'

Julie sighed.

'Oh, very well. By now I was properly awake. I put on my dressing gown and began to go downstairs. But Paul was already down there. He told me to stay where I was. He said something dreadful had happened.'

Mrs Talbot closed her eyes.

'Then I saw Bernard lying there...I just screamed and screamed. Paul came up to comfort me. Then Major Briggs arrived. The front door must have been open. He told us not to touch anything and he called the police.

'Did he use his mobile?'

'No. I don't think he has a mobile. He went back to his house to use the landline.'

'And what did you do while he was making the call?'

'I sat on the stairs. Paul went down to the kitchen and made some tea. I'd just joined him in the kitchen when Briggs returned. He told me to go and get dressed. He would wait outside for the police to come. By the time I'd dressed that constable – Blount was it? – had arrived.'

She paused, trembling, as she remembered the scene.

'Paul fetched some blankets and we just sat in the kitchen.'

'Did you ask him why he'd come downstairs earlier?'

'Yes. He told me that when woke he had this feeling that something had happened downstairs so he went down to investigate. He saw his father lying there. He thought he heard the latch click on the back door so he went outside but it was too dark to see anyone. When he came back in he saw me coming down the stairs. Then Blount arrived. And then you two came. The rest you know.'

'And you can't think of anyone who hated your husband enough to kill him.'

Mrs Talbot hesitated, as if considering the possibilities. Then shook her head and muttered, 'No.'

Dundee suddenly changed tack.

'Mrs Talbot, you say you didn't want to leave Birmingham and move out to the Moss. I gather that Mr Talbot took a cut in salary to change his career. Were things difficult, I mean financially.'

'No. Not at all. That's the strange thing. Suddenly Bernard seemed to have plenty of money. He bought a new car. A Range Rover. Brand new. Of course he needed that sort of car for his job. But I know they cost a lot. And he bought new clothes for himself. Really good stuff. Tweeds and so on. And he gave me much more housekeeping. Oh, and an expensive ring. We ate well. I could have bought myself a complete new wardrobe. But what would be the point, living out there?'

Jack and Dawn both looked puzzled by this revelation. Had it got any connection with all the cash in that bag? They were certainly going to have to take a careful look at Bernard's bank account.

The investigation had suddenly taken a new turn, but there were no more questions for Mrs Talbot at present. 'Interview concluded at 11.45 am.'

Dundee turned off the recorder.

Mrs Talbot stayed in the room while they interviewed her son. He seemed even less affected by his father's death. Dawn thought him a cold fish. Tall and pale as if he had outgrown his strength. She also reckoned he was probably gay, but so what, thought Dawn.

Paul spoke calmly and clearly. He confirmed his mother's description of events and the detectives learned nothing new. It was obvious that he disliked leaving Birmingham as much as his mother, possibly more, and hated his new school. He knew about his mother's friendship with David Hurst and he emphasized that it was simply that, a friendship. He told them his mother had been very lonely since they came to live near the Moss and that his father seemed to work longer and longer hours, not coming home till late at night or the early hours of the morning, and recently he had become violent towards his mother. He seemed to tremble slightly when he mentioned this.

Paul said that he too had benefitted from his father's new affluence.

'It was almost as if he was trying to buy my love,' said Paul.

Dawn grimaced at this odd way of putting it. That seemed like a very mature observation from a teenage boy.

Soon the interview ran out of steam and mother and son were allowed to leave. Dundee and Eccles went to the canteen for lunch. When they were settled at a quiet corner table Dawn asked, 'So, Jack, what have we learned this morning?'

'Absolutely sod all,' said Dundee.

'Well, there's plenty of motive. She had begun to hate her husband and might have wanted him out of the way. His physical violence might have been the last straw.'

'But I really can't see her doing the deed. The doctor said that the killer would have to be quite tall. Julie...Mrs Talbot is certainly not that. And surely if she had killed him she would have been spattered with blood. They have found only a trickle in the house and the coat they found near the copse definitely belonged to a man. A man of average height, apparently.'

'What about the boy? He obviously had no great love for his father and when he saw him hitting his beloved mother that may well have tipped him over the edge. He's an odd lad anyway.'

'But murder! Do you think he's capable of that?'

'Well...What I don't understand is why the murderer carried the corpse back to the house. Perhaps they were trying to throw suspicion onto the wife and son. To stop us looking for someone else.'

'Yes, I suppose...

At that moment Dundee's phone trilled. It was Jane. Dundee smiled to hear her voice and told her that unless something else cropped up he and Dawn would meet them that evening at a pub in Ellesmere, which served good food. He gave her directions and they decided a time to meet. Jane was delighted, closed the call and went off to tell Patrick.

The day ended without any progress in the murder investigation. And there had been no sighting of Lesia or Darren. The bag had not been recognised by any of the shopkeepers or identified on the internet. None of the local banks admitted issuing the cash. The coat found in the copse behind Lilac Cottage was still being examined. Nothing that might have been the murder weapon had been discovered, even though the search had been widened. Briggs and Tom Perry had made written statements that merely contradicted one another with regard to the characters of Bernard and his widow. The occupants of the other cottage had not been found. That other corpse, the ancient one, had been taken to the laboratory of a forensic archaeologist for further analysis. If that man had been murdered they were a couple of millennia late in finding who'd done it.

So Jack phoned Leanne to tell her that he would be late as they were meeting up with Patrick and Jane in Ellesmere. He asked in a kind of code whether there was any news and when Leanne said there was none he became momentarily depressed. He asked if she would like to join them this evening, but she said she was feeling tired and would have an early night. Dawn had no one to report to, which made her sad, but the thought of a reunion with their old friends soon cheered her up again.

NINETEEN

'Bye, Leanne. See you tomorrow.'

Leanne gave a little wave as she closed the salon door behind her and stepped onto the Square. She took a deep breath. The air felt very fresh after the salon with its fetid air full of chemicals. But she loved working at Severn Waves as the salon was called. It had been great to get a job so quickly after the move to Shrewsbury. It was sheer luck that one of the experienced girls had just left to get married and move away. And the others were so friendly. She had expected resentment because she started on a good wage, even though she was new, and she was allowed to leave early each day to collect the twins from school. Of course her references had been excellent, she was fully qualified and she worked very hard when she was there. She liked everything about the job, even the customers. They were generally more affluent than at her old salon in Bridgeport and they expected good service. But it was their conversation she enjoyed: much wider topics and more thoughtfully expressed.

She crossed the Square and stood at the bus stop, waiting for the bus to Gains Park, the suburb where they now lived, right on the edge of town with a view of the south Shropshire hills. She began to hum one of her favourite melodies. She felt so much happier with her life. Her marriage to Jack had been improved by the move. She no longer feared the influence of that pretty young woman, Agnieska, who had now become a detective and moved to another force. She was so pleased to have Jack back safely after that business with the sex traffickers that she had made love to him with an abandon that she hadn't felt for years.

The move had been good for them all. Jack seemed thoroughly happy in the new force and had already had a couple of successes: catching a couple who were using false paperwork to gain entry into the homes of OAPs and nicking purses and jewellery and then he and Eccles had trapped an arsonist who was just about to set fire to another church.

The twins had settled easily into their new school. Sean was always sociable and found new mates almost immediately. Karen was a good pupil and her quiet, hardworking attitude was much appreciated by her new teachers.

Leanne liked the buzz of the county town, with its more interesting shops and dozens of cafés, especially that one near her now, which served the most delicious cakes, but she had her figure back at last and was determined to keep it, so she resisted temptation and stepped aboard her bus which had just pulled in. She settled into her seat, thinking life was pretty good. But there was a problem and now that she sitting quietly with nothing to do it came back to her forcefully again.

She'd missed a period and the next one was almost due. She was usually regular as clockwork. And she was feeling other symptoms of pregnancy. She had warned Jack of the possibility and he was as worried as she was. In their delight at being properly together again they had been particularly amorous of late and perhaps rather careless. The last thing they needed at this time was the expense of another child and the disturbance to their lives, especially at night, that came with a new baby. They were obviously both older than when the twins were born and Jack had a responsible and exhausting job. He needed his sleep. She had just got a job that she really enjoyed and the extra money was useful. The prospect of being stuck at home with a new baby and less money did not appeal at all.

Of course it might be simply what they called 'the change of life' but she doubted that. After all she was only in her late thirties. And she did not show the other signs that are supposed to go with that condition; she had not been feeling tired or sweating or getting snappy with Jack; in fact the very opposite.

Leanne knew that the obvious thing to do was to have a pregnancy test or visit her doctor, but she was reluctant to do this because she feared having the pregnancy confirmed. Stupid really, but they had so much to lose.

She got to the school gates just as the twins were coming out. She hugged Karen and they stood together waiting for Sean to break away from his circle of friends. They were good kids and she loved them to bits. The last thing they needed just now was an addition to their family.

TWENTY

When she woke Jane felt nauseous and made for the bathroom. Despite her discomfort she was delighted. She just knew she was pregnant, even though it hadn't been confirmed. Today she would have to tell Patrick, who still lay snoring away in the king-size bed. She drank some cold water and it seemed to settle her stomach.

On her way back to bed she looked out of the window and saw that the weather had changed completely. The sky was clear blue and the trees across the street were shimmering with frost. As she got back into the bed Patrick stirred, then slept again. The room was quite warm, but she still arranged her dressing gown around her shoulders as she sat up, adjusting the pillows behind her and picked up the guidebook from the bedside table.

There was a description of a place just outside the town. It was a hillfort called 'Old Oswestry' and according to the guidebook was one of the finest examples of such things in the country. Apparently it went right back to Stone Age times but its heyday was the Iron Age. There was an aerial photograph and the hillfort did indeed look impressive. On such a morning it would be good to climb to the top and enjoy the view.

In the dining room she tried not to look as Patrick wolfed down a full English breakfast. Jane dipped a croissant in her coffee and explained about the hillfort.

'That's a great idea, Jane. It's such a lovely morning.'

Patrick got directions from the receptionist and they set off. The frost had melted but they still wore their warmest clothes. The Porsche wound its way through the town centre, then they glimpsed what appeared to be a footbridge over a railway. Patrick had already discovered that the line had been closed since that vandal Beeching's time, but a small section of it was now being restored by volunteers.

They turned left along a terraced street which climbed to the edge of the town and continued as a narrow winding lane. Soon the hillfort loomed above them, in a series of banks and ditches. Patrick parked the Porsche in a lay-by. They crossed the lane and went through a kissing gate. There was a noticeboard which gave them some information about the fort, then they began to climb up a steep, well-made path, paved with crushed stones. By the time they reached the top they wished they hadn't worn so many clothes. The sun was shining down from a cloudless sky and the air was very still.

Patrick stood looking down into the banks and ditches.

'Can you imagine digging all that, Jane, with just primitive tools. Not a JCB in sight. It must have taken years.'

There was another noticeboard at the top showing them what the hillfort must have looked like back in the Iron Age. What it looked like now was the top of a large flat cake with a path running around the perimeter. They decided to go left.

'Think what it must have been like, living up here in those days,' Jane said. 'You would certainly see your enemies approaching from any direction.'

'And I expect those ditches were full of sharpened stakes,' said Patrick.

Another noticeboard showed them the settlement as it would have been, with a group of huts made of wood and thatch, and a stockade full of cattle and sheep.

As they walked along the path the uninterrupted view of the landscape was amazing. Looking westward they saw those hills they had seen from the castle mound and to the north there were higher hills and beyond those the purple tops of what might be mountains.

By the time they were halfway round the path and looking across the flat north Shropshire plain, Jane was hot and tired.

'Let's stop for a while,' she said and Patrick nodded. He laid his coat, which was waterproof as well as warm, on the closely nibbled turf. She removed her coat and sat down on part of Patrick's.

'Phew, that exercise had really warmed me up. I'm thirsty too.'

Patrick, like the middle-aged boy scout that he was, drew two small bottles of mineral water from his coat pockets and handed one over to Jane. As she gulped greedily from the bottle, she thought, well, here goes!

'Patrick, I've got something to tell you.'

He was gazing into the distance where a short blue and white train was running along a still used track.

'You've decided you've had enough of me and you want to run off with the milkman.'

She took his nearest hand in hers and squeezed it.

'It's you who might want to run away. You see, I think I'm pregnant.'

It took a while for her words to sink in, then Patrick turned, grinning and hugged her.

'Oh, Jane, that's fantastic news.'

Patrick said nothing else for a while. He seemed to be considering the implications of what she'd told him. She just felt blissfully happy and her eyes filled with tears. Suddenly Patrick frowned and spoke again.

'But should you be climbing up steep banks in your condition, Jane.'

She laughed. 'Oh, Patrick, it's very early days. It hasn't even been confirmed.'

'Yes, but...'

She stood up.

'Come on. Let's walk on round.'

The rest had cooled them down, after all it was only February and the air was still cold, so they put their coats back on and walked around the other half of the perimeter. Birds were busy in the gorse bushes in the nearest ditch and a rabbit crossed their path, rushing to safety among the bracken, its white tail bobbing.

They met two couples, both with dogs, walking the opposite way round. Jane wanted to share her news with them, but managed not to be so foolish, commenting on the weather instead.

At last they completed the circle and stood at the top of the path leading steeply back to the road. Patrick took Jane's arm and helped her down as if she had become fragile. She didn't object because the stones of the path were quite slippery from the melted frost.

When they reached the lane Patrick suddenly went rigid.

'Shit! Where's my car?'

It was true. There were two other cars in the lay-by now, but no Porsche.

'The bastards! I didn't even fix the wheel lock. I never thought about thieves out here.'

'Oh, Patrick, that's dreadful. You'd better call the police.'

A patrol car arrived fairly quickly. It must have been a quiet time for crime in Oswestry. Patrick explained about the missing car. The young woman constable radioed into the station with a description and the registration number and an alert was set up.

'Can you remember,' she asked, 'exactly where you were parked?'

Patrick showed her. It was slightly to the left of where the other cars were now parked, which indicated that the Porsche had probably still been here when the others arrived. Her companion, a rotund middle aged guy, sweating in the sun, pointed at the ground. The lay-by was wet and rather muddy. There were clear tyre prints from a wide wheeled car.

Patrick nodded. The tyre prints went on along the narrow lane, in the opposite direction from where they'd come.

'How long ago did you park the car?' asked the man, wiping his brow.

Patrick looked at his watch.

'About an hour ago. D'you reckon that's about right, darling?'

Jane blushed. He'd never called her that before.

The police officers gave them a lift back into town, first to the police station, where all the details were recorded. Then they made their way disconsolately back to the hotel for lunch. Even the news about the baby couldn't quite dispel Patrick's gloom about losing his car. It wasn't new, by any means, but it had been looked after like a baby, until now.

Lunch was a sombre affair. Patrick was still grieving for his car and Jane suddenly felt very tired. They both just pecked at their food then Patrick went off to hire another car so that they could continue to explore the district and go to meet their old friends that evening.

Jane went back to their room to lie down. When she fell asleep she had a disturbing dream. She was back at her father's funeral. When she peered over the edge into the grave it wasn't the body of that young girl lying on the soil but a baby, wriggling and squealing. Jane quickly clambered down into the grave and held the baby in her arms. Suddenly the grave around her began to collapse and she and the baby became buried in soil. She panicked and began to push herself and the baby out of the grave. At that point she woke, with her heart thumping and her limbs covered in sweat. Gradually she calmed down and realised that the room was far too hot and that she had become tangled in the thick duvet.

She got out of bed and showered. Feeling much better Jane put on fresh clothes and sat at the dressing table to comb her hair. There was a single grey hair among the brown and she quickly tugged it out. She would have to start dying her hair. She couldn't have her baby seeing her with grey hair.

TWENTY-ONE

They couldn't see much of the little town of Ellesmere when they drove in as it was already dark. Patrick had kept muttering about the hire car as he'd driven the few miles here. Of course it was a perfectly nice little car, but it wasn't his Porsche.

'No oomph at all. You can't hear the engine. I don't feel like I'm really driving.'

Jane sat back smugly and said nothing. That afternoon she'd bought a test and her pregnancy had been confirmed. Soon they would be seeing their old friends and sharing a meal in some 'olde worlde' pub. She was bursting to give them her news.

When her pregnancy had been confirmed the first person she wanted to tell was Tony. He had become more of a father to her than her own. In spite of his severe arthritis Tony was always cheerful and full of fun. He had won the lottery a few years ago and bought a splendid house at the edge of a village in Kent. Last year it had become their base while they were involved in uncovering the sex-trafficking business. The house had been large enough for Dundee, Eccles and Grabowski to stay there as well as poor Peter Staines, Patrick and Jane. She knew that Tony would be delighted to hear about her pregnancy.

But her telephone call went unanswered. She was very surprised, knowing that Tony rarely left home and when he did he always took his mobile with him. She wondered if he might be ill, or had been involved in an accident, but Patrick told her to stop worrying and to call him tomorrow. 'He's probably got a problem with his phone, that's all.'

They found the pub and parked behind it. Her sickness seemed to be confined to mornings and she was really hungry. The restaurant was not as she had imagined, because it wasn't in the old part of the pub, but had been built on. It was very bright and colourful and beautifully warm. And there were their friends, already sitting at a table for four, inspecting their menus.

Jack stood up and gave her a big hug. He was as tall and handsome as ever. Patrick gave Dawn a quick peck on the cheek. After the usual pleasantries they settled in their seats and Patrick announced, 'There's good and bad news. Which d'you want first?'

'Definitely the good news,' said Dawn. 'We've been dealing with bad news all day.'

'Oh yes,' Jane said. 'That murder. We saw it on the news.'

'So you saw the news conference we gave at Shrewsbury police station. Right, can we forget that business for the evening,' Jack said. 'So what's your good news?'

Patrick burst in before she could speak, his face alight with joy.

'My darling Jane is pregnant.'

'Oh, that's fantastic news,' said Dawn grabbing Jane's hand across the table and giving it a hard squeeze. 'Congratulations!'

Jack said nothing, but smiled wanly. Jane thought he went rather pale, but he soon recovered himself and congratulated her as well, then asked 'So what's the bad news?'

Patrick answered glumly, 'My Porsche has been stolen.'

Jack seemed happy to change the subject.

'That's bad luck. What are the police doing about it?'

'Everything they can. They seem to be quite efficient.'

'Strangely enough I've just heard about a case of car theft. This gang was taking quality cars and disguising them for sale on the Continent. But they've been caught. Perhaps there's another gang doing the same thing. You're staying in Oswestry aren't you? I'll have a word with a guy I know who's based over there.'

Dawn released Jane's hand, asking, 'So when's this baby due?'

She was about to answer, when a waiter came to the table asking if they were ready to order. She quickly told Dawn that her baby was due in October. Jane thought that Dawn sighed rather wistfully, but she felt hungry again and picked up her menu. Patrick asked the waiter to come back in a few minutes and babies and cars were forgotten as they planned their meals.

The food and wine were good and the company excellent. They talked mainly about that time last year when they had all helped to bring an end to that horrible sex-trafficking business. They toasted absent friends, Tony of course, and Agnieska Grabowski, the beautiful, brave young woman who had risked her life to infiltrate that evil mob and put Lord Oxendale – now stripped of that title – in jail for the rest of his life. Then they fell silent for a while, as each one thought about Peter Staines, who had given his young life to the cause. They drank their heartiest toast to young Peter.

Jane left the table to, as that stupid euphemism puts it, powder her nose. She passed through the bar on the way and caught reference on the television news to that murder. When she returned to the table she asked Dawn, 'What's it like? This Moss where the murder took place?'

It was Jack who answered.

'Strange place. Big flat open space. Nothing there.'

'That's rubbish,' said Dawn. 'It's a fascinating place. They are trying to return it to the way it was. There are plants there that don't grow anywhere else. And bodies have been found from two thousand years ago, preserved in the peat.'

Jack said mockingly, 'Dawn did a course.'

She ignored him and continued, 'Don't listen to Jack. It's well worth a visit. Just forget the murder and spend some time on the Moss.'

'I think we must,' said Patrick. 'That's if the weather stays good. And if you're up to it, Jane.'

She wasn't too keen, but thought it might take his mind off his stolen car.

'OK, we'll check it out.'

TWENTY-TWO

It was late when Jack got home. He took off his shoes in the hallway and crept upstairs. He peeped into the twins' rooms and saw that they were both fast asleep. He didn't turn on the light in the main bedroom but it was almost full moon and the curtains were open. Leanne's bare shoulder and one side of her face glowed in the moonlight and her blonde hair looked silvery.

'Is that you, Jack?'

'You're still awake.'

'Hmm. Just about.'

He took off all his clothes, got into bed, and held her close. Leanne grumbled, 'Brrr…You're cold.' But she didn't pull away.

'How are you?' Jack asked.

She knew what he meant. 'Just the same.'

Jack said nothing. He had hoped…But so be it.

'How were they? Patrick and Jane?'

'Fine.'

He laid his hand on Leanne's stomach and added, 'Jane is pregnant.'

Leanne put her hand on his.

'Wow! How does she feel about that?'

'Delighted.'

'It is Patrick's I suppose?'

'Oh yes.'

'But they're not married.'

'Who cares these days?'

Jack snuggled up to Leanne, partly to get warm, and partly because he felt suddenly close to his wife. Then he whispered, 'Patrick's car has been stolen.'

'I thought those car thieves had been caught.'

'It must be another gang.'

'Hmm. Was Patrick very upset?'

'I think the baby had taken his mind off it a bit.'

'Well, they've no money worries have they. It won't matter too much if Jane has to give up her job.'

Jack's hand continued to move over his wife's willing body. Leanne did not stop him but she said, 'Hey, remember, I'm a pregnant woman.'

'That's OK then. You can't get pregnant twice.'

Leanne murmured, 'We'll be all right, won't we? With another child?'

They said nothing for a while. Jack suddenly stopped and asked, 'But what if you're not pregnant and I...'

'Shush, Jack. Just get on with it.'

DAY THREE

TWENTY-THREE

The weather remained bright but chilly. It suited Leanne's mood as she made her way to work. Last night's gentle lovemaking had been very fulfilling. Her worries about the pregnancy had faded and she felt herself glowing with health and smiling at everyone as she boarded the bus for the town centre. Even the traffic seemed to be flowing well this morning and she was soon leaving the bus in Market Square.

As she crossed the sunlit square she was surprised to see someone sitting on one of the benches so early in the day. At first she thought it was a homeless person. Even in affluent Shrewsbury this was sometimes a problem. She often saw men, and occasionally women, huddled in shop doorways, or using cardboard boxes as shelters, with little dogs asleep beside them. She wondered how they had become homeless, thanked her lucky stars that she had never been in their position and dropped a few pound coins into the hat or tin beside them.

But when Leanne went over to give the person on the bench a pound or two she realised that the hiking gear and rucksack were far too new and clean for a down and out and as she looked closer she realised that the woman bending forward to study a map was actually someone she knew.

'It can't be.'

The woman looked up. Leanne thought she had matured in the year or so since she had last seen her. It was not that she looked older exactly, but perhaps wiser. Her fine features had sharpened and there was a touch of sadness in the eyes, but as soon as she smiled the old Agnieska returned. That smile was captivating. No wonder, thought Leanne, that Jack had been tempted. And how lucky she was that he had resisted temptation.

'Agnieska!'

The young woman continued to smile.

'Leanne! Well, well. I'd heard that you and Jack had moved to Shrewsbury. But I never thought...'

Leanne sat down on the bench beside Agnieska and asked, 'What are you doing in Shrewsbury? I thought you worked in Birmingham now.'

'That's right, but we've been very busy. Some leave came up so I thought I'd get out of the city for a while. I'm catching a train to Whitchurch soon, then I'm going to walk along the Llangollen Canal towpath for a few days, staying in B & Bs along the way. I decided to have a quick look at Shrewsbury between trains.'

'That sounds great. Get out and about while you're single and free.'

There was a slight twinge of regret as Leanne said this, thinking that she might soon be tied down by another child.

'You're looking very well,' said Agnieska. 'Positively blooming.'

'Thank you.'

'There is another reason for my getting right away. I had a relationship that went sour.'

'Ah,' said Leanne. 'Man trouble.'

'Yes, indeed. How's Jack, by the way? And the twins?'

'They're fine. Jack's working on a murder case, with Dawn. The kids have settled into their new school really well. I've got this job at a salon just round the corner.'

She checked her watch.

'And if I don't get a move on I'm going to be late. It's been lovely to see you, Agnieska. Why don't you come and see us, on your way back to Birmingham. What's your phone number?'

Leanne entered it into her own phone, saying, 'I'll send you our address. Bye now. I must rush. Enjoy your hike.'

She gave Agnieska a quick hug, got up from the bench and hurried away.

Agnieska sat for a while, thinking about that difficulty at the station. She had really thought that her career might be going somewhere, but the guy concerned had turned out to be a shit, not only trying it on, but becoming quite nasty when she confronted him. Perhaps one day she would meet someone like Jack and settle down with a couple of kids. But, as Leanne had suggested, Agnieska liked her freedom and loved her job, or at least she used to.

She looked up at the clock on the old market hall and realised it was time to make her way back to the station to catch the train to Whitchurch. What she hadn't told Leanne was that this hiking holiday wasn't just a chance to get away for a while and be free from that man. She was working for the drug squad now and she was following up some information they'd been given about a group operating somewhere out in the sticks. If she could make progress with this it might improve her image back at headquarters, and she certainly needed that.

TWENTY-FOUR

Day had come at last. Chinks of light showed through the shutters. The power had run out some time ago but the boat was still reasonably warm. Lesia and Darren had begun to relax a little. The big guy had left them alive. Their wrists were becoming sore from the ropes tied around them but with their fingers free they had been able to drink from the bottles of water. Darren had tried to undo the ropes around his wrists and ankles but couldn't get enough purchase on those expert knots with just his fingers. Best of all, thought Lesia, that weirdo Piggy had gone away. He had given her the creeps. But soon they would be released, perhaps later in the morning or early afternoon. They had tried shouting for help a few times but to no avail, but it was obvious, as the big guy had said, that no one came near such a backwater at this time of the year. They exercised their limbs as much as they could with wrists and ankles tightly constrained.

At first Lesia had been angry with Darren, and told him so. He had used the wall behind him to force himself upright, then shuffled across to Lesia and told her he was sorry, but explained again that he had been forced to take these drastic measures just to be with her.

Lesia said nothing for a while but she had begun to accept that Darren really did love her. He had arranged this whole elaborate abduction thing, which had gone so disastrously wrong, to tell her that he loved her, because the restraining order made it impossible for him to talk to her in the normal way. She had also begun to accept that Bernard may well have been a criminal, as Darren had suggested. Those late night visits to the Moss were certainly strange and Bernard did seem to have much more money than his modest salary would suggest.

She would have liked to study those pictures on Darren's phone again but the big guy had taken it with him.

She began to feel very tired, after her broken night and the release of tension after that disgusting Piggy had gone away. Her eyelids began to close and she began to doze. Darren was pleased to see her sleeping. She needed it. So did he, but first he needed to check out their situation. Perhaps there was a way they could escape before those villains returned.

First he checked the cabin, in the dim light, in case there was something he could use as a tool, but there was nothing. Even if he could break a window, there were those sturdy shutters on the outside. The boat had obviously not been used for some time. There were no utensils or knick-knacks. Even the lid of the stove, now cold enough to touch, was hinged in place.

He worked his way awkwardly across to the door which led to the deck and pulled on the brass knob but it was firmly fixed and the door was solidly built, and anyway he didn't want to wake Lesia. He slowly shuffled across the cabin to the other side a few inches at a time, nearly losing his balance but the cabin was small and there was always something to lean on. He entered a corridor of shiny wood. On one side was a toilet, thank goodness. With his fingers he managed to unzip his jeans and relieve himself. Next to the toilet was a small bedroom, with a narrow mattress on a base, but the cupboards beneath it were empty. He thought that the kitchen – didn't they call it a galley on a boat? – would be next but the door to that was firmly locked. Shit! There would probably have been all sorts of useful things in there, like a knife.

His painful progress around the boat had exhausted him so he lay down on the mattress in the little bedroom and soon fell asleep. When he woke again it was dark. Oh no, it was night again and they hadn't been released. He felt very thirsty and his stomach was beginning to grumble with hunger. He lay in the dark, thinking what a bloody fool he'd been and realising that there was no way now that Lesia was going to return his love. It was obvious that those guys were not going to come back and release them. Something must have gone wrong. He had got Lesia and himself into this mess. He had to get them out.

He lay back in the dark and began to think what he could do. Then he became aware of a sound from the main cabin. It was sobbing. Lesia was crying. Oh hell! He struggled to his feet and shuffled next door. Between sobs Lesia was muttering something about the darkness getting to her and how she used to be claustrophobic. She thought she had conquered it but now…

His eyes had almost become used to the dark, but Lesia's black skin merged with the darkness, so all he could see was the whites of her eyes and her perfect teeth. He used his free fingers to gently stroke her face and she stopped sobbing. He told her about the toilet next door if she needed it, and that he would help her to reach it.

Darren tried shouting for help again but soon realised that no one was going to be near them in the dark to hear him. So he saved his energy for helping Lesia get to the toilet, then he returned to the main cabin and considered his next move.

He took the cushions from the seats on either side of the cabin and manoeuvred them side by side on the floor and laid the duvet on top. When Lesia returned she could hardly see a thing. She called out, in panic, 'Darren, where are you?'

'Down here.' He patted the mattress. 'I've made a bed.'

'Well, don't think I'm lying down with you. You've done enough damage already.'

'Look, Lesia. It's obvious they ain't coming back. Something's gone wrong. There's nothing we can do now in the dark, so let's rest until it's light again. Then we'll find a way out, or we'll shout until someone comes by and gets us out. Come on, babe. Just lie down and try to sleep. We'll be nice and warm and we'll be OK in the morning.'

'I suppose...'

Lesia lowered herself onto the mattress beside Darren, and snuggled under the duvet. He made sure not to molest her in any way. They just lay quiet for a while, then Darren felt Lesia shift her body closer to him, for warmth probably, he thought, and he wished his arms were free so that he could hold her.

'Darren?'

'Yes, babe?'

'We will be OK won't we?'

'Sure, Lees. Just try to sleep.'

He felt her snuggling closer again. Then she became still. Soon they both fell asleep.

TWENTY-FIVE

The detectives managed to locate the occupants of the remaining cottage. They discovered that the young couple, originally from Latvia, were working at a smart hotel just north of Oswestry, so Eccles picked up Dundee early next morning and they made their way to the hotel at speed along the A5.

The young immigrants were very frightened when the detectives turned up at the hotel and asked to interview them. Naturally they thought it had something to do with their right to be in the country, but their papers were all in order. Once the couple, Matis and Inga, realised that the police were not there to deport them but to ask about another matter altogether they became helpful enough.

Because of their long shifts at the hotel they rarely did more than sleep at the cottage and the day before yesterday they hadn't returned at all after their night shift. Instead they'd gone to join some friends in Wrexham to celebrate the birth of their first baby. When they finally came back to the cottage the police had already left so they didn't even know that a murder had taken place. Of course they were shocked when DI Dundee informed them, and they were very surprised when they learned that it was Mr Talbot who had been murdered. Bernard had been the friendliest of their neighbours and had always smiled and said hello on the rare occasion that they met. Yes, they had occasionally heard the sounds of a quarrel next door, through the thin walls, but surely all couples argued from time to time.

They had been living at the cottage for a few months but rarely saw the other inhabitants. Inga had tried to be friendly with Mrs Talbot but she had been rebuffed. And Matis said that he thought the boy was rather strange. He had seen him peeping through the bedroom window when he was exercising in the garden.

The husband and wife were a handsome couple; he was tall and slim, with black hair and dark eyes. Inga, his wife was rather petite, with blue eyes and fair curls. She had learned to speak English very well and her husband was making some progress. They liked Eccles immediately and Matis explained that they wanted to earn enough so that they could return to Latvia before too long and set up a small hotel of their own somewhere on the Baltic coast.

Inga explained that they had never seen the old couple in the middle cottage, but they gathered that the woman was an invalid and her husband was her carer. The man in the end cottage was thoroughly unfriendly. He had gone red in the face when he first saw them and told them to go back to wherever they came from, so after that they made sure to avoid him.

Usually the young couple worked the same shifts and travelled to and from the hotel in a battered old Nissan Micra. They had rather envied Mr Talbot's splendid Range Rover and assumed he had a well-paid job in one of the nearby towns. He obviously worked long hours because they'd sometimes seen him come home very late or even early in the morning.

It was soon obvious that the couple had nothing useful to tell them about the murder, but hearing about it Matis became worried about Inga's safety and his English began to fall apart as he tried to express his concerns. Eccles assured him that the murder was a one-off event in a generally crime free district and that there was no madman roaming about the Moss killing innocent people. As she smiled and tried to convince Matis she realised that she wasn't really so sure. After all, this murder did seem motiveless and very brutal. What if? No, don't go there, thought Dawn.

The young Latvian couple agreed to come into the station next day and each make a written statement. Luckily it was their day off and Inga thought she might like to do some window shopping in the county town. Dundee found the manager and explained that the questioning of the young couple had been purely routine and they were not involved in any way with the crime being investigated. The manager seemed very relieved, 'Thank God for that,' he said. 'They're such damn good workers. I'd hate to lose them.'

As the detectives drove back towards Shrewsbury Dundee suddenly asked, 'So who do we reckon murdered Bernard Talbot?'

The A5 was quiet at this time of the morning so Eccles had time to think as she drove. After a pause she suddenly said, 'Everyone we've spoken to says that the boy is strange. And it's obvious he preferred his mum to his dad. But would he have the courage to kill?'

'Well, Jones said the murderer had to be tall. The boy is certainly tall for his age. And if he'd seen the father abusing his mother...I do think we have to speak to him again. Put him under pressure. He certainly had the opportunity and he might well have had a motive. Yes, he's the most likely suspect, I agree.'

Eccles considered this then said, 'But was little Mrs Talbot in cahoots with him? Was he doing her dirty work?'

'You really don't like the woman, do you, Dawn?'

'The whole set up strikes me as distinctly fishy. I noticed that love bite on Mrs T's neck, and she was friendly with that teacher.'

'Yeah, and I think the murder took place much earlier than the lad said. According to Jones, rigor had begun to set in.'

'So you think that business of someone going out of the back door was a lie.'

'I do. But then what about this Darren character. Where the hell has he gone? And has he got anything to do with Lesia's disappearance? Did she have anything to do with the murder?'

'The whole thing's a muddle. We badly need a breakthrough.'

'I agree. Hey, let's go back to the cottage now, while we're reasonably fresh and have another look at that Moss place behind it. We might get a new point of view.'

Dawn was really pleased to hear Jack being so positive and committed again. He must have had a good night's sleep. She slowed the car.

'OK, I think we can go through Ellesmere if we turn left here.'

TWENTY SIX

Most of the time Paul hated this place. He could never understand why his father liked it so much. There was nothing here. Just this great big open space. The wildlife lot had ripped out most of the trees. Just left the copse at the edge and a few low bushes, usually full of noisy birds as soon as the sun shone. And the drains had been stopped up so the whole place was saturated. If you missed the paths you could easily slip into pools of nasty freezing black water. As usual there was a cold wind, from the north Paul reckoned, but at least the sun was shining this morning. He knew his way around pretty well. He came here when he wanted to think. And he was glad to be out of the house today.

The police had finally gone. They'd poked and pried into everything. Made a right mess of his room. All the time asking, 'What's this for? Why have you got that?' 'For Christ's sake, I'm a teenager,' he wanted to say. 'I like that kind of music. It suits my view of life. And gay mags! Just one or two. For fuck's sake. I'm stuck out here. The only boys I see are at that crappy school. And they think I'm a weirdo or a wimp. I have needs like any other lad of my age. Sometimes I just have to let go.'

And his mother had become very strange. He had thought she would be glad to be rid of her husband. He'd become cruel to her. Knocked her about. And Paul when he tried to interfere. You'd think she'd be glad to have him out of her life. Now she could marry David. He'd make a great dad. They got on really well. He was also into art and books and music. But now Dad's dead she seems to have changed her mind. It was Bernard this and Bernard that. All the time.

Of course finding him dead on the floor like that was a terrible shock for his mother. But Dad probably deserved it in a way. They both knew he was up to no good. He never came home till really late. His pockets were full of cash. He didn't even notice when Paul pinched a few quid. And he was always offering to buy him stuff. And Mum. He kept getting her this expensive jewellery. But he never took her anywhere to show it off. And look at that car. Top of the range. No way could he have afforded a car like that on a warden's wages. Would have cost an arm and a leg. Definitely a babe wagon. Oh yes, Paul knew there was another woman in it somewhere. His father had always had an eye for other women and the younger the better. Yes, it was much better that he was dead. They would both be happier now.

God, he used to bore Paul to tears. All that stuff about nature, conservation, global warming. Mind you, he could do with a bit of that now. The sun's bright enough but the wind's like a knife. He should have worn a thicker coat, but he just wanted to get out of the house. Be on his own for a while.

Perhaps they could go back to Birmingham soon. They certainly didn't have to stay here, now that his father was dead. Just give it a week or two until things settled down. Then David could leave his wife and get together with Mum and they could all move to Birmingham.

Hey! What was that over there? Something in the grass was catching the sunlight. Paul went over to look. What the...? It looked like a hammer. Inside a plastic bag. A small hammer. Like the ones in the craft room. It was quite heavy. It fitted his hand perfectly. Shit! What was that on the head? It might be blood. Dried blood. It was smeared on the inside of the bag as well. Christ! thought Paul, this must be the murder weapon.

Suddenly he heard someone behind him.

'Hey, Paul. Wait a minute. We'd like a word.'

Who on earth...? Oh no, it was those detectives. Paul thought he'd better get rid of the hammer.

He dropped it back on the ground. He didn't think they had seen it. He waited for the detectives to catch up. Surely there was nothing wrong with going for a walk on the Moss.

'Hello, Paul. What are you doing out here?'

'Just walking. Thinking.'

'Got a lot to think about haven't you?'

Paul didn't like the way the man said that. It was DI Dundee. Dundee! Like a fucking cake. Brain full of currants. Paul smiled at the idea.

Then the other one, Eccles was it? Another fucking cake! 'What was that you just threw away, Paul?'

Paul reckoned she was the sharp one.

'Nothing. Just some rubbish.'

'It looked like something metallic to me. You stay with Paul, Jack. While I have a look. Can't have him littering the Moss.'

Paul began to blush. Perhaps he should run away. He reckoned he could out run them both.

Eccles had that hammer. She was lifting it carefully by the very end of the handle between two fingers.

'Well, DI Dundee. What do you think of this?'

She dropped the hammer back into the plastic bag.

'I think, DS Eccles, you may have found a very important piece of evidence.'

Paul began to explain, 'It's not mine. I just found it. Wondered what it was.'

The man looked at him and smiled.

'I think, young man, you'd better come along with us.'

He grasped Paul's shoulder. It hurt. He hadn't realised how strong the man was. He decided he'd better do what the detective inspector said.

TWENTY-SEVEN

It seemed to take ages for them to get going next morning. Jane and Patrick luxuriated in their warm bed while the world started up outside. Then of course Jane felt queasy and had to sit in the bathroom while she brought up the remains of last night's meal.

When she looked out of the window it was quite misty but the mist had a sort of glow and you knew it would soon melt away and leave another sunlit day. So long as they wrapped up well it would be a good day to explore another part of north Shropshire.

Patrick had gone back to sleep. Poor thing, thought Jane. He's getting too old to be a dad. She slipped in beside him and dozed again for a while. Then she heard the clock from the church opposite strike nine and realised that they were going to miss last breakfast unless they got a move on.

A quick shower together and they just made it downstairs. Another full-English for Patrick and a croissant and coffee for herself. Jane wondered how Patrick could eat so much and never get fat.

'So what's the plan today?' she asked.

'Well first I'm going to take that piece of junk back to the car hire firm and get a decent motor. God, how I miss the Porsche.'

'I wonder if Jack will have any news?'

'I doubt it. It's not even his patch really.'

'I thought he seemed worried about something last night.'

'Well that murder was a nasty business.'

'I thought it seemed more personal than that. I hope he and Leanne are getting on all right.'

'Not much we can do about it.'

'No. So how long will this car business take?'

'No more than an hour. Then we'll make for that place Dawn recommended. Something Moss.'

'Whixall. Yes, it sounded quite unique. And it's not far away. We can have a pub lunch afterwards.'

'Good idea. Let's get going.'

So Patrick left for the hire place and Jane did a bit of shopping. Before she left she phoned Tony again, but his phone was still dead. She checked the number in her diary just in case. It was fine. She rang again. Still nothing. Oh well, she'd try again this evening.

The shopping took ages because every time she met someone with a pram or pushchair she couldn't resist having a look and a chat.

Eventually they set off, driving through Whittington, with its castle and moat resplendent in the sunshine, then a long climb up to a village called Welsh Frankton – an indication of how close to the Welsh border they were – followed by a long descent into Ellesmere, pulling in briefly beside the Mere with its crowds of geese, ducks, gulls and a few swans, gathered at the water's edge like holidaymakers on the beach at Brighton, all preening themselves in the sunshine.

They turned on to the Whitchurch Road and a few miles further on took a right turn down a much narrower road, very muddy in places, where they needed to drive slowly while she studied the directions Dawn had given them, because this little car had no satnav. The only traffic they met was a couple of tractors, which they manoeuvred past gingerly while they waited in field gateways, the drivers giving them curt salutes as if saying, 'What the hell d'you want to come this way for?'

At last they reached the place Dawn had recommended for the start of their walk on the Moss. There was the classroom, empty now, where the students would have gathered for their courses with that man who got murdered. Jack and Dawn had given them a brief account of the events of the last couple of days. Jane couldn't help but think of Bernard lying in a mortuary somewhere and of that girl who had just disappeared into thin air.

They parked the car, put on boots, buttoned up their coats and set off down a track leading into a dark wood. Here the trees grew so close that the sun could hardly penetrate. Many of the trees seemed to be decaying, so that their dead limbs rubbed together, making eerie sounds. They walked on along what seemed to be a causeway with wide ditches full of black water on either side. A dead branch had fallen in to one of the ditches and it resembled a large snake lifting its head as if to strike. Jane shuddered and wished they hadn't come to this place.

Suddenly the trees ended and they came out onto a wide open space, with a wall of dark conifers in the far distance and an ominous bank of purple cloud gathering on what Patrick said was the western horizon. They would have finished their walk long before those clouds reached them, he'd said.

They walked on along the causeway, the sunlight dazzling off the many pools of dark water and the air full of birds flickering from the alder or willow bushes.

'What an extraordinary place,' Jane said.

'Like the Russian Steppes,' Patrick answered. 'I could quite expect to see a gang of Cossacks come riding out from those trees, like that scene in *Doctor Zhivago*.'

Patrick loved those old films. Jane didn't bother to tell him she'd never seen it.

They reached the place where a sort of grave had been dug in the peat. It was surrounded by tape as if it was a crime scene. The hole had already begun to fill with water.

'That's probably where they found the ancient corpse,' said Patrick. Dundee and Eccles had told them about that amazing find.

Jane felt herself giving another little shudder. Then she realised that a cloud had suddenly obscured the sun. She was very glad she wasn't alone out here, and grabbed Patrick's arm.

'Come on,' he said. 'Let's walk on a bit, then get back for lunch.'

Since the sun had gone behind the clouds the character of the place had changed completely. Now it seemed bleak and desolate and a cold wind rose, chilling Jane's cheeks. Last night she'd read about the peat cutters in the old days and tried to imagine what it would have been like for them working out here in all weathers.

They increased their pace and walked on silently for a while. Patrick pointed out a pair of buzzards hovering above them in the strengthening wind, like those eagles they had seen on a trip to northern Spain, in the foothills of the Pyrenees, as they drove towards Pamplona. They had gone first to see Felicia, a Spanish girl, whose boyfriend, Peter, had been killed during the capture of that sex-trafficking gang last year. Felicia was still grieving but happy to stay with her uncle and aunt near Santander, and make a new life for herself. Wow, thought Jane, we could badly do with a bit of Spanish warmth now.

She saw a large bird sitting beside a wider, cleaner looking pool, like an old fisherman, half asleep but waiting patiently for a catch. As they approached the large bird, a heron, lumbered into the air, its wings flapping ponderously as it lifted into the sky.

That cloud they had seen approaching now covered the whole sky and it had become so dark that the horizon was quite indistinct. Jane looked back and realised that they were more than halfway across the Moss. Suddenly it began to rain, quickly becoming a real downpour.

'We need shelter,' shouted Patrick against the wind and rain. 'It's too far to go back. Let's make for those trees.'

So they ran on as fast as they could, remembering her condition, and as they approached the dark wall of pines they could just make out some buildings half hidden among the trees.

'Looks like a farm,' said Patrick. 'Perhaps they'll let us shelter for a while.'

Water was beginning to trickle down Jane's neck so she ran on with renewed vigour. Soon they'd be out of the rain.

At last they reached the buildings and stood gratefully under the eaves of a large shed or barn. The farm, if that is what it was, seemed to be deserted. There were no lights on anywhere and the place was silent. There were no farm implements in sight and no animals to be seen or heard. Not even a dog or a cat.

They stayed under the eaves until the rain stopped. Then they began to explore. There had only been a low fence as they came in from the Moss. Jane supposed visitors rarely arrived from that side, but they discovered that there was a sturdy fence and a strong gate on the other side, where a lane led away, probably to meet a proper road. The gate was padlocked and when Patrick climbed over he told her there was a large sign hanging from it saying 'Danger! Keep Out!'.

'Sounds like no one is welcome here' he muttered, as he climbed back over the gate.

They walked around the complex of buildings. It had obviously once been a busy farm, with a large Victorian farmhouse, and a number of outbuildings, barns, byres and such-like and, although it was deserted, it was all very clean and tidy, as if had been used for some other purpose until fairly recently.

At last they came back to the first building where they had sheltered earlier. Patrick sniffed and said, 'Do you smell that?'

Jane took a sniff as well. 'Peardrops?'

'Yes, very like that, but I reckon it's spray paint.'

Now he was really curious. He walked around to the front of the building, where there was a sturdy, padlocked door. For a respectable, law abiding businessman, Patrick has a strange collection of implements in his pockets. Now he took one out and inserted a thin strip of metal into the padlock, which suddenly shot open. He carefully opened the door, just enough to let in some daylight, weak though it was, and peered inside.

Jane followed him into the building and as her eyes became adjusted to the gloom she saw a number of vehicles covered with tarpaulins, and only recognisable as cars from the wheels below the tarps, and in one case these had been removed so that you could see the axles and brake drums only.

'It's a garage,' she suggested.

'Or a workshop,' said Patrick.

He lifted the tarp off the nearest car. 'Wow!' he said. 'Whoever this place belongs to is very well heeled. That's an Aston Martin.'

He walked to the next car and lifted its cover.

'Shit!' he exclaimed. 'That's my car. Look.'

Jane moved closer and agreed with him. The registration plates had been removed but there were marks on the upholstery and a scarf on the passenger seat that made it instantly recognisable.

'Right, let's get out of here quick and back across the Moss. We've obviously discovered the car thieves' hideout. Have you got your phone? I left mine in the hire car.'

Jane took her phone out of her pocket, but at that moment a deep voice behind them said, 'Don't move, either of you, and drop that phone on the ground.'

As she looked up Jane saw two ugly looking men, and the muzzle of a revolver pointed at her chest.

TWENTY-EIGHT

Agnieska left the train and started walking towards the centre of Whitchurch along a road appropriately called Station Street. She had studied her maps and knew that her walk along the canal started on the other side of the town. She called in at Tesco's in the centre and bought some rye bread, goats cheese, a couple of apples and one of those energy drinks that had far too much sugar, but she didn't need to worry about her figure just yet. It was incredible how you could get anything you wanted in a supermarket these days, even out here in the sticks, as her colleagues would call it. This would keep her going until she reached her first stop that evening, a pub recommended in her guide. It was only eight miles away so she should manage that easily before it got dark.

She continued along the High Street, past a big old sandstone church, and on into the western suburbs. She walked well. She was young and fit and had the right gear, especially her boots which were already well worn in. Her pack was quite light, holding just a couple of changes of clothes, a book and a notebook, as she intended to stay overnight in good hotels or B & Bs. She expected the whole walk to take no more than four days.

This break from routine was essential. She needed to forget what had happened since she moved to Birmingham, especially DI Prentiss, the bastard. But this wasn't entirely time off from work. They had received information that something drug related may well be happening in this part of Shropshire. If she kept her eyes and ears open she might just pick up something useful. And she badly needed something to enhance her reputation as a detective, to compensate for the harm done to her career by Prentiss. That fucking man, she thought, as she strode along.

She'd found it hard at first, moving from a quiet area like Bridgeport to a real inner city district. The pace of life was so much quicker and the amount of violent crime almost unbelievable. Her parents had tried to dissuade her from going for the post but she really wanted to be a detective and there was little chance of that in south Shropshire. Of course she had been given good references and her appearance in the media over the sex-trafficking business meant that she was given the first post that she applied for.

Then there was DI Prentiss, who said he would take her under his wing. At first she was happy to accept his paternalistic hand on her shoulder as he showed her the ropes. He was of that older generation, she thought, who had not learned to be politically correct in their relationship with women. And he was helpful to her and full of praise when she had an early success. But then the hand on the shoulder became a touch on the waist. She seemed to be called into his office more than anyone else and after one interview he patted her bottom as she walked out.

Prentiss was not an ugly man, probably when he was younger he would have been quite handsome, but now he was overweight, his skin was poor and he gave off a whiff of body odour when he exerted himself. Things came to a head one evening when Agnieska was on night shift and there was no one else in their section. He asked her to come to his office and as they studied a chart together he put his arm around her waist and gave it a squeeze. Agnieska had exclaimed.

'I'm sorry, sir, but if you do that again I'll have to report you.'

Prentiss pulled away, his face went purple and he almost screamed, 'Out! Now!'

After that, everything changed. There were no more discussions in the DI's office. No more smiles on his sallow face. Comments were made via female officers about the unsuitability of her dress, skirts too short, trousers too tight, etc. Paperwork began to grow like fungi on her desk. And often it was returned as incorrectly completed, though she knew perfectly well that it was not. If she was sent out on an investigation it was with someone who disliked her recent fame and made damn sure she was not allowed to be properly involved, and the cases were often of the most trivial kind.

Agnieska wondered whether to complain to a higher ranking officer, but she knew that as a relatively new recruit complaining about a long serving officer she had no hope of being listened to. She knew what it would be.

'Prentiss? Come on. He's just being friendly. He's of that generation that likes to show his feelings in a physical way. You have to remember he's got teenage kids. Loves his family to bits.' And so on.

There was one consolation. There was talk of him being promoted to another division. Someone on high had put in a good word. She had a choice. Put up with it for a few more months, or try for another transfer. No, she'd stick it out. She'd do whatever she was asked to do, and as well as she could. But thank God for this short break. She bloody well needed it.

She reached the canal and set off down the towpath. The sun was shining, although there was a ridge of dark cloud up ahead. There were no narrowboats actually moving along the canal, but plenty moored, with smoke rising from their funnels, as the brave folk who lived permanently on the canal prepared their lunches. She admired the way these boats were painted and the clever names printed on their sides, such as *Firkham Hall* and *Aboat Time*. Piles of firewood were stacked on the roofs of some boats and tubs of bulbs were beginning to open on others. One or two of the boats had solar panels, to catch the meagre sunlight and others had satellite dishes for their TVs.

Occasionally a dog would bark as she walked past, and some of the larger breeds lay sleeping on the roof in the sun. They would give her a glance as she walked by and wag a tail in desultory fashion. She checked her map at the next bridge and knew that she was progressing well, so it was time to look for somewhere to sit and enjoy her lunch. And that cloud had moved much closer so perhaps she should take out her waterproof coat just in case.

In fact the rain came sooner than she expected, a few drops at first and then a torrent, so she ran for shelter under the next bridge and stood there, beneath the neat Victorian brickwork, while the rain beat down in frenzy on the unprotected canal. She had the shelter to herself, so she sat on her waterproof coat, with her legs over the edge of the towpath, and ate her lunch. Soon she was joined by a flotilla of ducks, who had decided that the weather was not as lovely for their breed as it is usually described. They advanced in formation and noisily demanded a share of Agnieska's lunch. She broke off a few small fragments of bread and chucked it towards them. This caused a rumpus of quacks and splashes so she told them there was no more. After a while they got the message and as the sun had come out again they swam on their way along the canal.

Soon Agnieska was able to return her waterproof to her backpack and set off towards her evening destination.

TWENTY-NINE

'Interview with Paul Talbot timed at 15.30 on Wednesday 23rd February. Those present, Detective Inspector Dundee, Detective Sergeant Eccles, Mr Paul Talbot and his legal representative, Ms Phyllis Marsh.'

Dundee began the questioning by asking, 'Did you tell us the truth about when you found your father's body?'

But instead of answering this question Paul asked, 'Why isn't my mum here?'

'She said that she wasn't feeling well enough,' said Ms Marsh. 'But she was happy for me to represent you.'

'What's wrong with her?'

'The murder business has got her down. She's feeling very stressed.'

'So it doesn't matter to her that I've been arrested. I could go down for murder.'

Eccles broke in, 'You haven't been arrested, Paul. You are here voluntarily. To answer a few questions.'

Paul turned to Ms Marsh. 'Is that right?'

'Yes, and remember you don't have to say anything if you don't want to. Just say "No Comment".'

'Right, let's start again,' said Dundee. 'Tell us about when you found your father lying on the floor.'

'I told you. When I woke up I sensed something had happened...so I went downstairs and there he was...dead.'

'And you heard someone leaving through the back door.'

'Well I thought I did.'

'And you went to look outside?'

'Yes.'

Eccles asked, 'Did you see anything?'

'No, like I said, there's these trees at the end of the garden. You could easily disappear among them. And it was still quite dark.'

At that moment there was a polite tap on the door of the interview room and a young police constable entered, looking embarrassed at having interrupted the interview.

'Mm...A message for Detective Inspector Dundee. Urgent they said.'

'Police Constable Edwards has entered the room. Interview suspended.'

He took the note and nodded to the PC to leave.

'Thank you, Edwards.' Then he opened the paper, read the message, smiled and passed the note to Eccles, then said, 'Interview resumed at 15.35.'

Dundee addressed his next comments to Ms Marsh. 'Just to keep you in the picture, Ms Marsh, this note is from forensics to say that the hammer found on the Moss is covered in Paul Talbot's fingerprints. Have you anything to say, Paul?'

Paul remembered that they had taken his fingerprints as a matter of routine when he and his mother had come to the station to make written statements. 'Of course my fingerprints are on the hammer. I picked the bloody thing up, didn't I?'

'You saw it lying there on the ground and you picked it up.'

'Well, I saw this thing shining on the ground, inside a plastic bag and wondered what it was.'

'Did you notice anything else about it?'

'Not at first. Then I saw something that might have been blood on the hammer head. I was horrified and chucked it away again. Then you arrived and brought me to the station.'

'Whose blood did you think it might be?'

Paul glanced at Ms Marsh. She shook her head. Paul said, 'No comment.'

DS Eccles asked, 'Didn't you think it strange to find a hammer on the Moss?'

'No comment.'

'You threw it away when you saw us coming. Why?'

'No comment.'

Dundee suddenly changed tack. 'Did you kill your father, Paul?'

Paul was obviously beginning to enjoy this.

'No comment.'

Ms Marsh stood up. 'I suggest we take a break. I would like to talk to my client. Perhaps you could arrange some tea for us both.'

Dundee and Eccles were reluctant to take off the pressure, but Ms Marsh had every right to stop the interview whenever she wanted, because Paul had not been cautioned.

'Very well,' said Dundee. They left the room and asked PC Edwards to arrange tea and biscuits for the solicitor and her client.

The detectives went to Dundee's office for a discussion about the interview so far, but when Jack sat down at his desk he found another note from forensics. He read the note, muttered, 'Well, well,' and stood up again. He led Eccles back to the interview room. As soon as he got inside he said to Ms Marsh, 'I'm sorry to have wasted you time, Ms Marsh. Paul, we do not need to continue this interview. You may go.'

Eccles looked distinctly puzzled and Ms Marsh quite cross as she returned some papers to her briefcase.

'Come along, Paul. I'll take you home.' Then she turned to Dundee. 'I'm afraid we didn't drink the tea. It was stewed.'

Ms Marsh and Paul left the room. Eccles asked, 'What the hell was that all about?'

'That message from forensics. The blood on the hammer wasn't Mr Talbot's. They haven't found a match at all.'

When he returned to his office Dundee phoned Leanne.

'Any news?'

'No. Just the same. But don't worry. We'll cope somehow'

THIRTY

There were two men facing them, both ugly brutes, one with a gun in his hand. He was a big man, with shoulders like walls, a large head and a scarred face. The gun looked very small in his large paw, but Jane was sure he could fire it if he needed to. The second man looked like an overgrown schoolboy, his face showing a distorted smile, like a wicked leer. For some reason she was more scared of him than the older man, who asked, 'So what the fuck are you two doing in here?'

Patrick managed to remain calm as he answered. 'We got caught on the Moss in that downpour. We came in here to shelter.'

'But the door was locked.'

'No, it wasn't. Someone must have been careless.'

'So what have you seen in here?'

'You have some amazing cars. Quite a collection. I've had one or two classics myself in my time.'

He didn't mention the Porsche, but went on, 'I suppose you do them up and sell them on.'

The short, plump young man's smile widened as he nodded his head. The older one muttered, 'Yeah, something like that...'

Jane was very frightened but managed not to say anything as Patrick explained, 'We wouldn't have touched the cars, you know, but I can understand your caution and your need for security. There must be half a million pounds' worth of stuff in here. Now the rain has stopped we'll just go on our way. We left our car on the other side of the Moss.'

'I'm afraid it ain't that simple. You see, I reckon you're not as thick as you make out. Soon as you're out of here you'll phone the filth and tell 'em about our "little collection" and they'll be round to check us out.'

The younger one nodded again. Jane began to wonder if he was all there.

'Right, Piggy, find some rope and tie them up. Just their hands will do. Oh and take any more phones off 'em. All of them. They can join our other friends on the boat, till we've shifted the goods to the new place. Then if I'm feeling generous I'll give the coppers a ring and tell 'em where to find you.'

The one called Piggy found some oily rope, probably used for towing cars and fastened it around Patrick so that he couldn't move his arms. Patrick had gone bright red with anger.

'You bastards. You're crooks. You steal these cars, change their identity, and send them abroad, where someone's waiting for them.'

'Ain't you the clever one. Worked it all out. Well by the time you're off the boat, if I decide to let you go, this little lot will have been moved on.'

Now Piggy turned to Jane. She smelt him as he came close. He was shorter than her but she felt very frightened as he grabbed her wrists and tied them together. He noticed that she drew back from him and held her breath. He gave the rope an extra tug and pinched her flesh. He felt in her pockets for a phone. Next some smelly rags were tied round their heads as blindfolds and they were pushed out of the barn and into a car. Piggy sat in the back with them.

The larger man spoke in a deep growl.

'OK, Piggy. Take the gun and if they try anything you know what to do.'

A metal gate whined open and they drove down a tarmac drive for a short distance before turning onto a smoother road. After a while they slowed down and made their way down a bumpy track. When the car stopped Jane sensed that there was water nearby. Piggy pulled her out of the car. The other man did the same to Patrick who, because he was much taller, caught his head on the car roof, and called out in pain.

Piggy pushed Jane forward again. She could feel his hand touching her buttock, and wanted to be sick. If her hands had been free, and she'd been able to see his face she would have slapped it as hard as she could. Now the blindfolds were removed because they had to step up onto the deck of a narrowboat, moored with two others in a sort of backwater off the main canal. The afternoon light was already fading at this time of the year. There was no sign that the other boats were occupied, but the one they were now standing on looked recently used.

The big man unlocked a door and Jane saw a short flight of steps ahead. He took the gun back from Piggy and pushed it into the small of Patrick's back. Then it was her turn to descend. She felt slightly dizzy and hoped she wouldn't fall down the steps and injure the baby. Thank goodness Piggy stayed back for a moment to close the door.

The cabin they were in was dark and the air was stale as if the room had been shut up for some time. The big man switched on his phone light and Jane could just make out two people sitting at the other end. One of them spoke.

'Have you come to let us out? Please let us go. Please.'

The older villain replied, 'Sorry, my dear. Change of plan. You got to stay a bit longer. These two are to blame.'

He moved closer to the couple. Jane could just make out in the poor light that both of them were black. She remembered Jack telling them about the case and realised who they might be but said nothing.

The older man spoke again.

'Tie the new ones to the benches, then come over here and tie these two up again. Can't have anyone wandering around, breaking the door down and contacting the coppers, can we. Mind you, that door's pretty solid and there ain't nothing in here they could use to break it down.'

'There's some tape in the car. Shall I get it and tape up their mouths?'

'No need. Even if someone does come along the towpath, and it ain't likely at this time of year, they won't come past here. They'll cross the bridge and go on towards Ellesmere on the other side. Hurry up now. We've gotta get them cars shifted. The boss is coming over to help us.'

By now Piggy had made them all secure.

'Right you lot,' said the older man. 'You can get to know one another. Have fun.'

He ushered Piggy up the steps, picked up his phone, followed the younger one up the steps and closed the door. They heard the lock turning. Now the cabin was very dark again. The young girl cried out in fear, 'Oh God!'

THIRTY-ONE

Dundee made an appointment to speak to Anisha Kaur, the new young pathologist, in the mortuary. The young Sikh woman had been appointed fairly recently but she had already earned DI Dundee's respect. But he had been perplexed by that note she had sent him about the hammer and surprised that the blood was not that of Bernard Talbot so he needed to check with her personally. He had long since ceased to be fazed by the sight of a corpse but the atmosphere of the mortuary still sent shivers down his spine.

Ms Kaur's smile as Dundee entered slightly softened her rather austere features with her dark hair pulled back in a severe style under her working cap and a pair of black framed spectacles. The lenses didn't seem particularly strong but they made the best of her large dark eyes, beautifully shaped and shining with intelligence.

'So you don't think that hammer was the murder weapon?'

'No. Well not this murder anyway.' As she said this she glanced at the body of Bernard Talbot, lying white and immobile on the bench, face down.

She picked up the little hammer in her gloved hands and placed its head near the wound in the back of Bernard's head.

'Do you see? The wound is larger than the hammer head. Even allowing for some splintering the hammer is too small to make a wound like that.'

Dundee moved closer as the pathologist placed the hammer head close to the wound and saw immediately what she meant. She looked up again.

'I've been examining the wound carefully and checking with things that might have been used.'

'Go on.'

'Well, that little hammer is the sort used for tacking something to a wall, like hanging up a picture, that sort of thing. But this wound was made by something slightly larger and probably heavier.'

'And your conclusion is?'

'The handle of a handgun? The murderer held the barrel and brought the handle down on the skull. Even a small handgun is quite heavy but I think this one was medium sized. Look.'

Ms Kaur went over to another table and picked up a handgun.

'I borrowed this from ballistics. Don't worry, it's signed for and it's not loaded.'

Dundee carefully took the gun from her. He reckoned it was a 9mm, slightly older style revolver, heavier than the really modern ones and with a longer barrel to get hold of.

'So why did you choose this one?'

'Let me show you.'

Ms Kaur took back the gun and holding it by the barrel placed the handle as close to the skull as she could without actually touching.

'Wow!' said Dundee. 'Nearly a perfect fit!'

'Yes, and the handle is quite solid. It would easily go through a skull.'

'Right,' said Dundee. 'So we're looking for a bad guy who owns a gun of that type. Now, what about the blood on that hammer head?'

'No idea, except that it's Group O.'

'Damn! That's almost half the population.'

''Fraid so.'

Dundee made one his customary, 'Hmms' and, 'Oh well, thanks for your help, Ms Kaur.'

'Do call me Anisha. You're Jack, aren't you?'

'That's right. Thanks again, Anisha.'

DAY FOUR

THIRTY-TWO

As DS Eccles crossed the Welsh Bridge on the way to Frankwell, with two uniformed officers in the back of her car, ready to begin house to house enquiries around Darren's last known residence, she noticed how high the river had become. She had seen photographs in one of the pubs of how it used to be, with people walking along planks built up on the pavement to allow them to get from the middle of the bridge to the higher levels of the suburb in comparative safety. The river wasn't going to flood just yet but she reckoned they would be getting the barriers ready pretty soon.

She sent PC Burnside to the right to begin knocking on neighbours' doors while she and Elaine Peters, a very new recruit, went the other way. Dawn would make the first few enquiries, then leave Peters to carry on.

Of course there was no reply at one or two places. People were out at work or shopping or not willing to answer the door when they saw Peters' uniform. But some of his neighbours did recognise Darren from a photograph, that had been sent by the force where he had lived in Birmingham, partly because he was black, which was unusual in this locality, but also because he was 'fit' as one young woman told them, meaning that he was physically attractive, but unfortunately none of those questioned had seen Darren in the last few days.

It was slow tedious work, as most police enquiries tended to be, so Dawn was glad when Peters said that she was confident enough to continue on her own. Dawn told her that she would be having a quick coffee in a local café and radioed Burnside to say the same. They would give it an hour or so and then return to where they had left the car.

Dawn found a small, recently opened café, and took her coffee, a remarkably good Americano, to a corner table and picked a newspaper – one of those not requiring much time or effort to read – from the rack. She was about halfway through the paper, which consisted mainly of celebrity gossip, when Burnside appeared at her table with a rather scruffy young man at his side.

Burnside informed DS Eccles that the young man had seen Darren the day before yesterday. Dawn ordered him a coffee and sent the PC off to find his colleague and tell her to return to the car, then she asked the man, who said his name was Raymond Skidmore, but everyone called him Skids, to sit down and tell her what he knew.

'Yeah, well, like, I seen him day afore yesterday. Thing is like, he was in a car. Posh car it were an' all. Didn't know he could drive, let alone afford a car like that. When I saw him he was just passing slowly, like he was looking for somewhere to park.'

'And you're sure it was Darren?'

'Oh yeah! Me an' him is good mates, like. Had a pint or two with him down the Wheatsheaf see.'

'Do you remember the make of the car?' asked Dawn.

'Oh yeah, I'm good on cars, like. It were an Audi. Black. Not top of the range but pretty near.'

'You don't happen to remember the registration?'

'Not all of it but the first bit stuck because I thought it was strange. See it were DN, like it were personalised for Darren. Then it were 09. That made it a year old. But I don't remember the rest.'

'And you didn't see him again.'

'No. I ain't seen him since.'

'Well, thank you very much, Mr…er…Skids. You've been very helpful. Where can I find you, if we need to speak to you again?'

'My flat, well it's just a room really, s'over there. No 7 Riverway, but I ain't in usually, like, 'cause I'm looking for a job. But you can find me down the Wheatsheaf, any time after six.'

Skids finished his coffee and hurried away as if it wasn't a good idea to be seen spending too much time talking to coppers.

It was raining as Eccles left the café and the sky looked as if it was about to burst. As she made her way back to the car Dawn considered what 'Skids' had told her. So Darren had a car, or had borrowed one. He had been seen in it the day before yesterday, which was the day before the night that Lesia disappeared. This meant that if he had kidnapped Lesia, or she had gone willingly with him, they could be miles away. This information was useful but also made their search for the girl more difficult. Anyway, with part of a registration they might be able to locate the owner of the car. She suspected it wasn't Darren. No way could he afford an expensive car like that.

Eccles phoned Dundee, to pass on her news, but his phone went straight to voicemail. Strange. He may be a bit of a technological dinosaur but he always had his phone with him and usually answered straight away. She called the station and asked to speak to him. She was told that DI Dundee had gone home. Some kind of emergency. They couldn't be more specific.

What the hell is going on? thought Dawn, as the three of them returned to the station.

THIRTY-THREE

Dundee drove back to the station from the hospital, where the mortuary was based, thinking about what he had learned. If, as Anisha Kaur had suggested, the weapon that had killed Bernard Talbot was a handgun then his killer was almost certainly a criminal. And if Mr Talbot was mixed up with criminals, his death was almost certainly connected with something illegal, whatever that might be. Well at least that let little Mrs Talbot and her strange son off the hook. Perhaps?

But what about Mr Talbot's pretty little assistant? Where the hell was she? And what about this Darren guy. Had he kidnapped the girl? And had either of them got anything to do with the murder of Bernard Talbot? Bloody hell, what a mess.

He had just reached the station when his mobile trilled. He expected the call to be from Eccles, who had gone to Frankwell to do a little house to house. But he didn't recognise the caller's name and he didn't recognise the woman's voice.

'Could I speak to Jack Dundee?'

There was something about the voice that worried Jack straight away. There was a sense of panic in it. And the fact that she didn't ask for DI Dundee. This was more personal.

'You're speaking to him.'

'Oh, Jack, I'm so glad I've caught you. This is Beryl from Severn Waves.'

For a moment Jack was confused. What on earth was Severn Waves? Then he remembered, and caught her panic.

'Is...is this about Leanne?' His mind was filling with thoughts about accidents: sharp scissors, poisonous chemicals, dangerous customers.

'Yes, Jack. She wasn't well. I took her to A & E at the Royal Shrewsbury. But I had to come back. We've no cover today. But don't worry, Jack. It's not life threatening. Well at least not for her. But she'll need your support.'

By now he was shaking but he tried to speak calmly to this Beryl who, he remembered now, was Leanne's boss.

'I'll go straight away. Thanks, Beryl, for letting me know.'

Hell! He'd just come from the hospital. He didn't have time to tell anyone where he was going. He drove as fast as he could through the town without putting any other road users in danger. He thought once or twice about using blues and twos because the town centre was busy as usual, but at last he was going up the Copthorne Road and would soon be in sight of the hospital. He did use his privilege of being a policeman to claim a spot in the A & E car park and hurried in.

A & E was heaving as usual. A large proportion of the patients being elderly, sagging in their chairs and looking like death warmed up. As he looked around for Leanne, he noticed one or two youngsters, with bandaged arms or legs, probably accidents at school, and a middle aged man so drunk he would have difficulty standing up. But no sign of Leanne. The few doctors and nurses were all busy, but he stopped a nurse in her hurried course across the tiled floor and asked, 'Do you know where my wife is? Leanne Dundee?'

At first the young woman looked blank. Her mind had been on another mission. Then she remembered.

'Oh yes. Lady with blonde hair. She's down there. Third booth on the left. There was a woman with her but she had to leave.'

Dundee was beginning to realise what might have happened. He tried to walk calmly down the corridor, but his heart was pounding. He pulled back the curtain. Leanne was sitting in a chair with her head bent low. When she looked up and saw Jack she smiled but he could see tears glistening on her cheeks. She put up her arms and pulled his head down to hers.

'Oh Jack…Jack.'

They hugged in silence for a moment, then Jack pulled another chair into the booth and sat beside her.

'You lost the baby?' he asked.

'Oh, Jack, it was awful. I was just doing someone's hair when this pain…terrible pain…I rushed to the loo and saw the blood. Great gouts of it. Of course I knew what was happening. The pain eased a bit and I called Beryl. She was brilliant. She asked Angela to take over my customer. Then she brought me straight here. But she had to get back.'

Leanne went silent and it was obvious that she was in pain again Then she relaxed and went on.

'Jack, it was awful. I had to wait for ages. Sitting there with all those people and blood running down my legs. Then they moved me in here. But I'm still waiting to be seen.'

At that moment a young nurse peered in. She was pushing a wheelchair.

'Mrs Dundee. I want you to come along with me. Doctor's going to check you over. Then we'll clean you up and take you to the ward. We need to keep you under observation for a while.'

'How long will she be in?' asked Jack.

'Oh, don't worry, I'm sure you'll be able to take her home tonight. We're always short of beds.'

The girl smiled, her face creased into dimples, making her look very young, but the way she helped Leanne out of her chair and into a wheelchair seemed very experienced and professional.

'Shall I come with you?' asked Jack.

'No, go back to the waiting room,' said the nurse, whose name Jack noticed from her name tag was Debbie. 'I'll call you when she's ready, then you can go up to the ward together.'

Debbie began to push the chair along the corridor. Reluctantly Jack returned to the waiting room. It was even busier and there was nowhere to sit. It seemed an age before the young nurse reappeared with Leanne in the wheelchair pushed by a white coated orderly. She beckoned to Jack and he followed the orderly, who seemed reluctant to speak, to a lift and then out into a ward, where one bed remained unfilled.

Soon Leanne was settled and they were alone. She was very pale and obviously tired. He thought she might have been given something to ease the pain.

Leanne lay back on the pillow and whispered, 'Well, Jack, the baby's gone. We don't need to worry any more.'

Jack leant over the bed and hugged her. They both sobbed. Jack muttered,

'Oh my love.'

Then Leanne's eyes closed and she slept.

THIRTY-FOUR

When Jack got back to the station he was met by an irate Dawn Eccles.

'Where the hell have you been, Jack? And why haven't you been answering your phone?'

'Sorry, I couldn't use it where I was. I forgot to turn it on again.'

'So where have you been?'

Dawn noticed how pale her colleague was and began to back off a little. Dundee said, 'Come into my office and I'll fill you in.'

Jack sat behind his desk and Dawn took the seat opposite. She noticed that his eyes were moist as if tears were close.

'So what is it, Jack?'

'I don't want this to become common knowledge.'

'You know me better than that, Jack. Go on.'

'It's Leanne. She's had a miscarriage. I went to A & E to be with her.'

'Oh shit. I'm so sorry, Jack. I had no idea she was pregnant. How is she now?'

'She's on the ward. Very tired. But OK.'

'Oh, Jack, I thought something was troubling you. But I never guessed.'

'It was an accident. We didn't want another child. But if it had happened we would have loved it like the twins.'

'I know that. You're good parents. I'll probably never know that feeling but...'

Dawn was feeling rather low herself. All these women getting pregnant. It was never likely to happen to her. Partly due to her sexual orientation, but also because her relationships never seemed to last. Would she like a child? Would she be a good mother? Her own childhood didn't offer much hope. Her mother had left them when Dawn was eight years old. Her father had cared for all three children by himself. She and her dad had been very close. As the oldest child she had become a stand in mother and helped him as much as she could. It had been a real struggle. Her dad could only work part-time and with three kids...They had lived in a small terraced house in a northern town. Even before her teens Dawn had cooked, cleaned the house and done the washing. The amazing thing is that they were a really happy family. Her dad appreciated his daughter's help, and the little ones tried to do as much as they could, though sometimes it would have been easier for Dawn if they'd just let her get on.

Her younger brother and sister were fine. They just accepted the situation. Sonia was the brainy one and was doing well at school. Brendan, named for his father's Irish roots was very musical, always singing or playing a guitar. Dawn loved them very much. Those were happy years.

But in her late teens two things went wrong, at least as far as her dad was concerned. Firstly she discovered that she had feelings for other girls, rather than boys. Secondly she became interested in joining the police force. By this time her brother and sister were old enough to cope for themselves. She decided to come out. Big mistake! Her dad was horrified. The others were puzzled but not too bothered. After all she was their big sister and they looked up to her, though they did not share her sexual feelings.

It became clear that Dawn was no longer welcome in her father's house. She loved him still, but he had made it clear he could not accept the way she was. So as soon as she was old enough she applied for the police. Again he was shocked and did not support her. However, she had done well at school, and had several Duke of Edinburgh Award certificates so the careers teacher at her school thought it was a very good idea.

Dawn was no beauty, but she was fit and healthy and had a strong social conscience. Her teacher persuaded Dawn's father that the choice of career was a sensible one. To be honest he was glad to see his daughter leave home and go to police college. She made a very successful recruit and soon had a satisfying affair with Stacey, a fellow student. Those were more good years too, though she still missed her dad, and kept a close eye on her siblings who both seemed to be doing well. Sonia was at Sheffield University by now, studying history and politics, and Brendan was becoming a successful musician in their local area, playing at local pubs and weddings with a small group who called themselves the Whistledowners after that lovely film with Hayley Mills.

Of course the affair with Stacey did not last, but by this time Dawn was a successful copper and had transferred to another force, where her talents were soon recognised and she became a detective. Before long she moved again and joined the south Shropshire force, where she was to partner Jack Dundee.

Now as Dawn looked across the desk at her partner she understood why he had been so distracted recently. He was a good man and a good detective. She was honoured to be his partner, even if he did have a weakness for pretty women.

Jack had closed his office door while he was filling her in about his problems. Now there was a curt knock and DCI Sturgeon swam in. This was a joke Jack and Dawn shared. Sturgeon was almost oval in shape and had this large flabby face, with full lips that were always moist. It was impossible now for them to see him as anything but a fish.

'Glad I've caught you both. I need an update on this Talbot murder and those missing black youths.'

They managed not to smile as Sturgeon sat in the chair that Eccles had quickly vacated. He was a heavy man and the chair creaked.

'Well, sir,' said Eccles. 'I was just telling Jack about my house to house over at Frankwell.'

'And?' said Sturgeon pursing his large lips.

'The guy, Darren, was seen in a car the day before yesterday.'

'Was he now?'

Jack pretended to have heard all this before.

'And we have part of a registration. The techies are working it.'

'So if this Darren took the girl she could be anywhere by now?'

'Exactly.'

'Damn!' exclaimed the DCI, flicking out his lower lip. 'And what about you, Jack? Any progress?'

'Well the pathologist thinks that Talbot was killed with the handle of a handgun. So I reckon we're looking for a criminal type for our murderer. It would seem that Talbot was mixed up with some lowlifes.'

'I see...This case gets more and more puzzling. Right, I want you both to get out there and make some progress. Otherwise I'm going to pull in some help. I'm giving you twenty-four hours. OK.'

With that the DCI rose, left the office and swam off down the corridor.

Dawn returned to the seat which felt very warm after the DCI had sat there. She asked, 'How long will Leanne be in hospital?'

'They think I'll be able to take her home this evening. But I'll have to collect the twins from school first.'

Dawn's phone rang.

'Hi. Eccles speaking.'

She smiled as she heard the message.

'That's great. Certainly sounds like a possibility. We'll give it a try. Thanks.'

Dundee looked puzzled. Eccles explained.

'It's the car that Darren was driving. They've found a black Audi with the right sort of registration. The owner lives in north Shropshire. Come on, Jack. If we go now you can be back for the end of school.'

The sky had cleared and the road was quiet as they left the A528 and turned onto the A495. They passed through a small village with a church on one side and a school on the other. Once they were through it Dawn put her foot down.

Dundee looked around, 'Haven't we been near here recently?'

'Yes. Look. There's the sign to Whixall. The Moss must be somewhere over there.'

She nodded to the right.

'Oh and here we are.'

Dawn turned the car into a smart driveway between tall white posts with a sign announcing 'White Gates'. Ahead of them they glimpsed a large stone house surrounded by mature trees.

'Very nice,' observed Dundee.

Several cars were parked in front of the house, including a black Audi. Dawn checked the registration number with the one in her notebook.

'Reckon that's it,' she said.

They moved to the front door and Dawn pressed the large brass doorbell. They heard it ringing somewhere inside. At last the door opened and an elderly man stood before them. They identified themselves and the man asked them to come in. He took them into a large drawing room, asked them to sit down and offered them drinks, which they declined.

'I rarely have a call from the police,' the man said. 'How can I help?'

Dawn asked, 'The black Audi outside, sir.' She read the number out. 'Is it yours?'

'Yes, though I rarely use it these days. I retired several years ago, you see, and my health is not so good. My name's Preston by the way. Simon Preston. Why do you ask about the car?'

'Has anyone else driven it recently, sir?'

'Well, my grandson sometimes borrows it. He's passed his test, but hasn't got a car of his own. He's a good driver. I'm happy to be driven by him.'

'Does he always ask your permission when he takes it?' asked Dundee.

'No, sometimes he forgets or can't find me, if he urgently needs to go somewhere. In fact he may have borrowed it for a couple of days. I saw that the car had gone yesterday. But it was back this morning. Shall I call my grandson and ask him?'

The old man dialled and his grandson answered. He said he had not borrowed the car yesterday. Preston passed on the news, with a frown forming on his bald brow.

'But something rather strange occurred this morning. The keys to the car were put through the letter box, with a note explaining that they had been found on the drive.'

Dundee and Eccles looked at one another.

'Do you have the note, Mr Preston?'

'Well I think it may be in that fireplace. Doreen, my housekeeper hasn't lit the fire in here today. The central heating has been enough.'

Dawn carefully extracted the crumpled note from the laid fire and put it in a plastic file. The old man's frown deepened as he watched.

'So what on earth is going on?'

'Well, sir, I think someone other than your grandson may have borrowed your car. Do you ever check the mileage?'

'Oh no, I never bother with that. And as I said I rarely drive the car myself these days.'

'Well, I'm sorry to say we may have to take it away for a while. Forensics will need to examine it.'

'Dear me! Will you be taking it with you?'

'No. A lorry will collect it, and return it as soon as possible.'

'I see. So what is this all about?'

'I'm afraid I can't tell you that,' said Dundee, 'but it is a serious matter. And we are very grateful for your cooperation.'

'Are you sure you won't have a drink.'

'No thank you, sir,' said Dawn. 'We must be on our way. But we'll keep you informed.'

THIRTY-FIVE

Agnieska had made good progress since the rain stopped and was well on her way to her evening destination. She had met no one on the towpath for the last mile or so. She supposed some people might feel afraid of being completely alone in this isolated area but she was a karate black belt and a police officer trained to deal with awkward customers. In fact she felt safer here than alone at the station with DI Prentiss. Shadows were beginning to deepen but the towpath still showed clearly and the surface of the canal reflected the fading light. She increased her speed to make sure of getting to her goal before nightfall.

Suddenly there was a blue flash among the undergrowth on the other side of the canal and Agnieska stopped to discover what it was. As she stood motionless looking across the water a small bird with beautiful blue foliage dived from a branch, caught something in its beak and flew back to the branch, where it turned the catch around in its beak and swallowed what appeared to be a small fish.

Agnieska knew at once that the bird was a kingfisher. She had never seen one in real life before but she had shared numerous wildlife programmes with her dad when she was younger. She thought how much he would have enjoyed seeing this bird, but since his wife, her mother, died he had become a bit of a recluse and not kept up his country walks. It was her father who had introduced her to canals as well, of which there are several around Northampton, where she had lived with her parents until she joined the police.

The bird did not reappear for a while, but then, there it was again, perching on that branch and peering into the water. It was so busy looking for its next meal that it did not notice Agnieska at all, even in her bright yellow kagoule. She took out her phone with the minimum of movement and snapped the bird on the branch. It must have noticed her slight movement because it suddenly disappeared. She waited a while but the bird did not return.

The light had begun to fade so she turned to walk on.

Shit! She fell heavily, gasping for breath and her ankle hurt like hell. When she looked down at her foot she saw what had happened. She had stepped into a mooring ring hidden in a tuft of grass at the edge of the towpath. Her fall had taken her breath away for a moment. She turned slowly and sat up. Pain shot through her ankle again. Christ I hope it isn't broken, she thought. Suddenly being in such a lonely spot did not seem such a good idea.

Well at least she had her phone. She'd put it back in her pocket after taking those photos of the kingfisher. She felt for it. It wasn't there. Perhaps it had fallen out onto the towpath. She looked around. No phone. Fuck. Oh fuck. It must have fallen into the canal and she hadn't noticed as she herself fell.

Pain surged through her ankle again. She took off her walking boot and sock. Wow! The ankle was already swollen. She felt the swelling and decided that at least the ankle wasn't broken. She could still move it very slightly, if she was prepared to put up with the pain. She put the sock and boot back on, fastening the laces as tightly as she could bear. Now it was time to try to stand. First she knelt then pressed down on the good ankle and stood up. She took a few steps. It was agony and she felt herself sweating, but she had to keep going, before the light disappeared. In fact it was already noticeably darker.

Agnieska struggled on for twenty yards or so. She came to a hazel bush and saw one strong looking branch in the centre. She took a little knife from her backpack and began cutting into the wood. The knife was sharp but small and it took ages but at last she had made a sort of staff and trimmed off the twigs. She set off again and found that leaning on the staff did help a little. Now it was almost dark. She came to a bridge which seemed to take the towpath onto the other side of the canal and was about to go that way, when she caught a glimpse of some boats moored in a sort of spur off the canal. Perhaps there would be someone on one of the boats and they would have a phone.

THIRTY-SIX

The lorry came to collect the Audi soon after DI Dundee and DS Eccles left Mr Preston and headed back towards Shrewsbury. This time Dundee was driving. For a while they rode in silence while Eccles tapped on her smartphone. She was always doing that, observed Dundee. When she'd finished she said, 'Well what do you think?'

'What do I think about what?'

'Preston.'

'Seemed nice enough. Obviously retired. He was a solicitor wasn't he? Poor health. Not many people would let the police take away their car without complaining. Why d'you ask?'

'I just checked him out. Yes, he's retired, or rather he was asked to retire. Apparently he left under a cloud. There was some suspicion of financial irregularity. Nothing proved but...'

'Any record?'

'No, nothing. I suppose I just thought he was very smooth. I don't like smoothies. Especially ones with big houses and expensive cars.'

'You're just jealous.'

'Yes, a bit. But it's not just that. I had this feeling about the man.'

Dawn could never entirely forget her impoverished childhood. Dad had been a miner until the coal industry collapsed. He managed to find other work, unlike so many of his colleagues, only part-time so his pay was a pittance compared with mining, and he struggled to keep things going for his three children when his wife left him because she said he'd become such a miserable sod. Dawn was incredibly grateful that her dad made her stay on at school, even when anything she could earn in some dead end job would have really helped. Now she was not welcome at home, and though she sometimes ached with love for her father, she could not return.

Back at the station both detectives went to their own desks to check on calls and emails. Then Dundee asked Eccles to join him in his office.

'Too soon for anything from forensics I suppose?' Dawn asked.

'Yes, but they've got the car.' Jack paused. 'That wasn't that I wanted to tell you about.'

'No? Is it Leanne?'

'She's fine. I have to collect her at six. Oh, and our neighbour, really nice woman, is collecting the twins from school and keeping them till I get back.'

'That's great. So what is it?'

'I just phoned Patrick to ask about the Porsche.'

'And.'

'No answer. His phone's turned off.'

'Perhaps they're having sex. Isn't this a sort of honeymoon for them?'

'But they were planning to visit Whixall Moss today. Not the sort of place I'd choose for a bit of nookie. So then I phoned Jane. Her phone's not responding either.'

'I see. Well I'm sure it's nothing serious. Leave it a while and check again. We don't want any more bloody disappearances.'

At that moment Dundee had another call. He put it on speaker so Dawn could share the call.

'Hi Jack, we've given the car a quick check. Luckily, we'd nothing else in. It's good news and bad.'

'OK, let's have the bad news first.'

'Who ever borrowed that car obviously wiped everything afterwards. Even the exterior door catches. Not a sign of any driver at all.'

'Damn!' said Jack.

'But.'

'Yes?'

'The good news is, we found some hairs on the back seat. Black hair. Afro-Caribbean type. Probably came out when someone was being forced into or out of the car.'

'Male or female? What d'you think?'

'I'd say female, but I can't be certain. I've passed it on to the lab.'

'Well done, George. That's a great help. I owe you a pint'

THIRTY-SEVEN

For a while they just sat staring at one another, Jane, Patrick, and the two young black people they could just make out in the gloom, then Jane asked, 'What are your names?'

The young man scowled but the girl said, 'I'm Lesia. This is Darren.'

'I guessed it might be,' said Jane. 'You see we're friends of DI Dundee and DS Eccles. They told us last night about your disappearance. So what on earth are you doing here, on this boat?'

'Well, you see...'

'No, Lees. Don't tell them. They'll tell the cops. Then I'll be in real trouble.'

Patrick said, 'If you don't want the "cops" to know. It's obvious you're involved in some criminal activity.'

Darren was about to say something crude, but Lesia stopped him.

'No,' she said. 'He's been stupid. Very stupid. But it's because he loves me. I understand that now.'

'I see,' said Jane. 'Well look, as we seem to be stuck here together for some time, you should at least know our names. This is Patrick and I'm Jane.'

There was a moment's silence while each of them considered their positions and wondered what they could do. Patrick said, 'We must try to get out of here and stop those bastards before they drive off with my car among others.'

'But what can we do?' said Darren. 'We're trussed up here like Christmas turkeys.'

'Yes,' said Lesia, 'and that horrible Piggy has tied the ropes much tighter this time.'

'Look,' said Patrick. 'There are four of us. We can at least shout as loud as we can. Surely someone will hear us.'

'Well we can try, but Darren and I have tried. We've been here for ages and we haven't heard anyone go by.'

'It's no good being negative. Come on, let's give it a try. One… two…three…Go.'

So they all shouted for help. The cabin practically shook with the sound. Then in the silence that followed they listened. Nothing! They tried again. Same result.

Jane felt quite out of breath. Patrick said that they should do the same every ten minutes or so. They all agreed. After all, what else could they do?

Jane had already decided that she liked Lesia. She wasn't so sure about Darren. She asked Lesia, 'You say that Darren brought you here because he loved you. What did you mean?'

'Don't, Lesia.'

But Lesia went on. 'Darren and I have known each other for quite a while. At first we got on well. Then he wanted to take our relationship further than I wanted to go, so we fell out. I came to Shrewsbury partly to get away from him.'

'That's enough, Lesia. You make me sound like a fool.'

'Are you telling me that what you did wasn't foolish?'

The young man lowered his head. He seemed ashamed. Jane's eyes were getting used to the poor light and she could see how pretty Lesia was.

'Anyway, Darren found me in Shrewsbury. He wanted to say sorry, but before he got a chance he did something wrong and had a restraining order slapped on him, so he couldn't see me at all.'

'Actually, I didn't do that thing. I asked a friend to put the frighteners on that guy Simon. I never meant him to touch the guy...But what's the point. If you're black you're bad.'

Patrick interrupted, 'That's nonsense. You've obviously got a chip on your shoulder. Anyway, it's time for another shout.'

So they all shouted as loudly as they could. But there was still no one to hear them.

Lesia looked at Darren and said softly, 'If these people promise not to tell their friends, will you tell them what you did.'

'I suppose. OK. So one of my neighbours – we sometimes have a drink together – told me about this boat. He couldn't afford to keep it, so he'd sold it to some guy who lives near here. For a lot more than it's worth. The guy said he was going to use it for groups to tour the canal. You know, schoolkids and disabled people. But when my neighbour came out here in the summer he discovered that the boat hadn't been touched. He asked the people on the other boats. They said they'd never seen anyone use it.'

Jane thought this was very strange. She knew that canal boats were expensive and then there were all the running costs. Why would anyone pay over the odds for a boat and then not use it? While she was considering this Darren went on.

'I began to have an idea. So I asked if I could use the boat for a couple of days. He said he hated to see the boat going to waste and gave me a spare key he'd kept. But if this other guy turned up I should just pretend to be homeless and looking for somewhere to kip overnight.'

Patrick told them it was time for another shout. They all groaned, but shouted anyway. Still nothing. No one.

'So what was this idea?' Jane asked Darren.

'OK, I know now how stupid it was, but I had to talk to Lesia. Show her how I felt about her. I came up here and made sure the boat was clean and tidy. Then I borrowed a car from a place nearby.'

'You mean stole a car!' said Patrick.

'I always meant to return it, and I did,' Darren snapped. Jane was pleased when Patrick remained silent.

'Anyway that night I went to her house and brought her here.'

'That's not quite what happened is it, Darren? You broke in…'

'No, the door was unlocked.'

'You came up to my bedroom and put something over my mouth, so I wasn't able to scream. Then you wrapped me in that duvet, put me in the car and brought me here.'

'So you kidnapped her,' Jane said.

'I suppose,' Darren replied, lowering his head again.

'But it's OK, Darren. I understand now. I know how much you love me. I'm glad we've had this chance to be together. But now I want to get out. I'm hungry and thirsty and getting cold.'

'Right,' said Patrick. 'One more shout. The loudest yet.'

They shouted so loud Jane reckoned they could be heard in Ellesmere. At first there was the usual silence, then they heard someone scrambling onto the boat before someone tapped on the door and asked, 'Are you OK in there?'

THIRTY-EIGHT

Paul couldn't make his mum out at all. She stayed in her bedroom, didn't even get dressed. She wouldn't even talk to him. She had hardly eaten anything and had gone very pale. It's as if she was feeling guilty about Dad, yet he knew she had had nothing to do with his murder.

The police hadn't bothered them again. Since that business with the blood on the hammer. Paul knew they had thought he'd killed his father. And there were times when he almost wanted to. Like when he hit Mum and when he showed his negative feelings about his son. That was because he was gay and not like his father at all. He kept making these sarcastic remarks. Yes, he hated him at times, but he could never have killed him, or anyone.

The strange thing is that his mother had made no attempt to see David, since Dad was killed. Paul thought she had loved him. He had begun to hope that she would leave Dad and go with David. But he hadn't even contacted her, so far as he knew. He supposed if he had he would have become a suspect. If the police thought they had a thing going.

Now he was very confused. Had Dad just been killed when he came downstairs? Or had he been dumped there some time before. There wasn't really that much blood. Perhaps he'd been killed somewhere else and what Paul had heard was his body being dumped downstairs. Did those who left the body there go out through the back door? Is that what he had heard? If he had heard anything. Now he wasn't so sure. And that blood-soaked jacket they had found. It certainly wasn't his. He would never wear a jacket like that. That wasn't his sort of gear at all.

The young people from two doors down had come round to say how sorry they were and was there anything they could do. They came from Latvia. Paul didn't really know where that was.

They had seemed really nice. He had made them a cuppa. They didn't have any biscuits or anything. Mum hadn't been shopping since it had happened. They chatted for a while, but his mum didn't even bother to come down.

And what was Dad doing to get himself killed. Paul had thought for ages it was odd the way he was always out so late and he had all that money. He'd got to the point when he was going to confront him, but then he was killed. Dad probably deserved it in a way. They both knew he was up to no good.

Mr Perry popped in as well. Paul had always felt sorry for him, having to look after his wife. She has that thing called Alzheimer's. Memory problems and that. Mr Perry wanted to speak to Mum as well but she wouldn't come downstairs.

Briggs hasn't been near them since the day it happened. Probably didn't want to get involved. Paul could tell he used to fancy his mum, dirty old man, but now she's been involved in a murder…

He hadn't been back to school since his dad was killed. They probably wouldn't mind if he didn't go back at all. Spoil their image, having a possible murderer among their pupils. He'd never really got on at that school. Those bullies had never left him alone. The other day they had come round on their bikes, just to gawp. Paul was upstairs, looking out of his bedroom window. Unfortunately they saw him and started shouting things, like 'fucking murderer' 'killed yer fucking dad'. Luckily his mother's room was at the back, so she didn't hear. After a bit they just went away again. What on earth the neighbours thought, he couldn't guess. He didn't care.

Paul got to thinking about school. He couldn't go back there, ever. He was really hoping that his mum would want to return to Birmingham. When this was all over. He hated most of the kids at his present school. And the teachers. David was the only one he liked at all. He was an excellent teacher. He had good discipline. Even those yobs behaved for him. He loved his subject and could make you interested. When he wasn't teaching he was usually in the storeroom, planning his lessons, but he was always happy to talk to Paul. He had gone to see him in there a few days ago. Before all this happened. David had his nose in a book as usual. But it wasn't an art book this time. He had this hobby, geology. He told Paul that Shropshire had a greater variety of geological features than any other county in Britain. Apparently he loved to go fossil hunting on Wenlock Edge. He offered to take Paul with him some time.

Suddenly Paul froze. He remembered what David had been twirling in his hand as he told him about fossils. It was a little steel hammer, just like the one Paul had found on the Moss. But the blood on the hammer wasn't his dad's. So whose?

THIRTY-NINE

'Help us please!'

Agnieska tried the handle of the door into the narrowboat's cabin but it was firmly locked. However, like most detectives, she kept a mixed bundle of keys in her pocket for such occasions.

'Hurry, please,' said Patrick.

Agnieska thought she recognised that voice but what on earth would Patrick be doing here on this boat?

At last one of the keys turned in the lock and she hobbled down the stairs. In the fading light she made out four people in the cabin but none of them moved towards her. Then she realised that they were all tied up. Suddenly a woman spoke.

'I don't believe this. Agnieska, is it really you?'

'Jane? What the hell's happening here?'

Patrick broke in. 'These bastards tied us all up so they have time to get away. We must catch them. We must call the police. Have you got a phone?'

'No. I fell over and it dropped into the canal.'

'Damn!'

Jane said, 'You fell. Are you in pain?'

'Yes, I thought my ankle was broken, but it's just badly sprained.'

'There's no time to describe our ailments,' said Patrick. 'We must catch those crooks.'

'Get these bloody ropes off me and tell me where to go for a phone,' said Darren. 'I'm a good runner. Leastways I was when I was at school.'

Lesia added, 'He was. Very good.'

'Luckily I didn't drop my knife,' said Agnieska. 'It's quite small but very sharp.'

She moved towards Darren. Patrick called out.

'Not him. He's in deep trouble. He'll just disappear.'

'That's not fair, Patrick,' said Jane.

Darren spoke angrily, 'What's the point of undoing you. You're an old man. You can't run.'

'Stop all this silly arguing,' said Lesia. 'I trust Darren. He won't let us down.'

Agnieska made her decision and quickly sliced through Darren's bonds. He massaged his wrists and twiddled his ankles to get the blood flowing again.

'Right. Where do I go for a phone?'

'Go back over the nearest bridge and turn left along the towpath on the other side. There's a village about a mile away. With a pub. They'll have a phone.'

Jane said, 'There's a piece of paper in my pocket. The numbers are for DI Dundee and DS Eccles. They're our friends. Just tell them we're in danger. Can you describe our location?'

'Yes. I brought Lesia here, like a fool, remember.'

'OK, get going. I want those bastards caught,' said Patrick.

'Don't we all,' said Jane.

Agnieska went round the cabin releasing the other captives. They heard Darren jump from the boat and begin to run along the towpath.

'Should we all get off the boat in case those guys come back?' asked Lesia.

'No, we must stay until Dundee and Eccles arrive.'

'They sound like a couple of cakes,' said Lesia with a smile.

'Maybe,' said Patrick, 'but they're excellent detectives.'

'Well, if those crooks do come back there're four of us to two of them,' said Patrick.

'Yes, but they're armed.'

'But they don't know we're free. And we've got surprise on our side.' Agnieska said.

'What about your ankle?' asked Jane.

'It's already less painful. I just need to rest it.'

'Come over here,' said Jane. 'Lie out here. Take off your boot and sock.'

'One of us should keep a look out, in case those crooks do come back,' said Patrick. 'I'll take first watch. Where's that key, Agnieska? We'll hear them unlocking the door, and we can be ready, but we need some weapons. I'll use your key to get into the kitchen and see what I can find.'

Patrick came back with a rolling pin, a carving knife, a large pair of scissors and a mallet for softening steak. Jane took the rolling pin. Patrick hoped that wasn't a sign of their future together. Agnieska took the knife. She had practised with one as a part of her police training. Lesia took the scissors, hoping she wouldn't have to use them. Patrick was left with the mallet. He practised wielding it a couple of times.

It wasn't too long before they heard Darren returning. He must have run like hell. Patrick unlocked the door to let him in. He told them that he had got through to Dundee and Eccles and they were on their way. Soon they heard a car draw up beside the canal. It seemed too soon for the detectives to have reached them, so Patrick put them in their positions, including Darren who had got his breath back and was itching for a scrap. They heard someone in heavy boots climb onto the boat and try the door. Lesia shook with terror. The others prepared to repel boarders. Someone tried the door. Then they called out.

'This is the police. Let us in.'

Patrick took the key Agnieska had given him and opened the door. Dundee came hurrying into the cabin, followed by Eccles.

'This is crazy. Patrick, Jane and, bloody hell, Agnieska. And Lesia of course. What the hell are you all doing here?'

Patrick burst in. 'No time for explanations. We have to catch those crooks. They stole my car and others as well. I can take you to their hideout. It's not far at all.'

'OK,' said Dundee. 'The rest of you stay here. Agnieska, you take my phone. If those guys come back call us. Immediately! Darren, you come with us.'

Jack thought Darren and would be very useful in a fight.

'When we've gone, lock the door, Jane, and don't worry. We'll have those monsters in custody in no time.'

Darren moved to follow Dundee but Lesia called him back, gave him a hug and kiss on the cheek, whispering, 'Take care.' Darren almost floated out of the cabin.

FORTY

Paul had been thinking about what might have happened. Perhaps David and his mother did plan the murder. They were in love and they wanted Dad out of the way. But now Mum was filled with guilt and she couldn't face David. It reminded him of a play they'd read at his old school, but he couldn't remember what it was called.

Now, in his mind's eye, he kept seeing David twirling that little hammer while he explained about fossils. He ought to tell the police but he was afraid of making things worse for his mother. Then he remembered that it wasn't his dad's blood on that hammer. That hammer had probably killed someone, but it wasn't his dad. So David wasn't the murderer. God, it was so confusing.

The other thing he began to realise is that Dad wasn't killed here in the house. There would have been a lot more blood than the trickle he had seen on the carpet. He had been killed somewhere else and dumped where he was found, in that position, as if he was trying to escape through the front door. But surely whoever killed him would have needed help? His dad was slim but not lightweight. One person couldn't have carried him far on his own. But who would have helped him do a thing like that.

Of course, he thought, that blood-soaked jacket found on the Moss. That's where the murder took place. That wasn't so far from the house. Two people could easily have carried Dad's body between them, so that there was no sign of it being dragged. But who had carried the dead body into the house and who had helped. If only he'd been quicker getting to the back door when he thought he had heard the latch drop he might have seen someone. But he was not sure now that he had heard anything.

At least he was no longer a suspect. Something to do with the blood on that hammer not being his father's. And he knew that his mother was still sleeping when he had found the body. So that left her in the clear.

He began to wonder who might have helped the murderer, and immediately discounted their young foreign neighbours. They hadn't even been aware of the murder until those detectives told them about it. And the old man with the doolally wife. There's no way he would have got involved with murder. Well, there was Major Briggs in the end house? Paul could tell he used to fancy his mum, dirty old man, but now she'd been involved with a murder...Paul couldn't see Briggs as a murderer or being involved with one. He was far too respectable. A magistrate and all that. And anyway he was quite an old man. There's no way he could have carried a dead body all that way.

So what should he do about all his suspicions? Should he go to see David and confront him? Perhaps he had nothing to do with the murder at all. It would mean going into school, which he dreaded. Or perhaps he could arrange to meet him somewhere else. Should he get in touch with those detectives and change his story? Perhaps they had already discovered something anyway. Or should he try talking to Mum? Somehow he thought that would probably tip her over the edge.

If only they could go back in time. Back to Birmingham. Before all this had happened.

FORTY-ONE

As Patrick led the way to the farmhouse Eccles checked her smartphone for a map of the area.

'The place is called Moss Farm,' she explained. 'It's in the middle of a copse, so we can easily approach without being seen.'

Dundee used his phone to call for backup. He gave the orders he had discussed with his colleague.

'Park your cars some distance away and out of sight. We don't know if these crooks are at the farm yet. By the way, wear your stun jackets. They're likely to be armed.'

When they reached the farm it was quiet. A quick tour showed them that the gang was not there. Half the expensive cars had gone from the barn. The wheels had been replaced on the vehicle that had been on the ramp and it was ready to drive. One of the remaining cars was Patrick's Porsche. He was checking it over, when Dundee's radio announced, 'Car approaching. Looks like an Audi. Black. Three occupants. All male. They've stopped by the gate. Two men have got out and opened the gate. The car is coming through. Shall we apprehend the driver?'

'No. We need to know where they've taken the other cars. If he drives off again tail the car. But take care not to be seen.'

Patrick, Darren and Dawn quickly hid in the dark corners of the barn and waited, except for Dundee. He stood in the open, ready to meet and arrest the men. He heard the large door of the barn creak open and there they were. The big man stopped and stared. Piggy was half hidden behind him.

Dundee began. 'I'm arresting you both for stealing a number of expensive cars and for the abduction of four people. You don't have to say anything...'

The large man laughed aloud.

'So you think you can arrest us, on your own, just like that. Bloody hell. You must be mad. Watch it, Piggy. There must be others.'

Piggy stepped from behind his partner. He had a gun in his hand.

'Get your fucking hands up, copper.'

At that moment something or someone flashed through the air and knocked Piggy to the ground, sending the gun flying. The big man was so shocked he just stood there facing Dundee as Eccles moved forward and slipped handcuffs on him. Piggy sat up on the floor, still dazed, as Darren picked up the gun and pointed it at him. He smiled as he said, 'I really enjoyed that,' then turned to Dundee and explained, 'He tried to touch up Lesia.'

Eccles pushed Piggy onto the floor, face down, and fixed another set of handcuffs on him. She realised he was just a wimp, all mouth and no balls.

Suddenly Dundee's radio burst out again, 'Man's just parked the car. He's coming into the barn.'

Dundee whispered to Darren, 'Keep the gun on the big man.'

The door opened a fraction and a man started to come in. Eccles exclaimed, 'It's that guy Preston. I knew he was a wrong 'un.'

The big man called out, 'Get out, boss. It's a fucking ambush.'

Preston went back out and put the bar across the door.

Again Dundee's radio crackled and a voice said, 'Suspect has come out of the barn and got into his car.'

'Can you tail him?'

'A couple have gone for their car but it's some distance away.'

Patrick shouted to Dundee, 'Get them to open up the barn. I've got my keys and she's ready to roll.'

Dundee gave the orders and soon the barn door was open. Patrick got in the driving seat and called to Dundee, 'Get in quick!'

Dundee jumped into the passenger seat, saying, 'Dawn, you sort things out here. We'll follow Preston.'

He spoke into his radio, 'Watch it! We're coming out.'

There was a deep growl and the Porsche leapt forward, out of the barn and down the drive. If they could get to the main road before the Audi turned they would know which way to go.

By now several members of the backup team had reached the barn and the two crooks were in custody. Darren handed over the gun. Dawn shook his hand, saying, 'Thanks, Darren. You were brilliant.'

FORTY-TWO

Agnieska stood near the door, knife in hand, listening intently for any footsteps on the towpath. She also had an ear out for the phone in her pocket. Please let the fruitcakes make a quick arrest, she thought, then we can get off this damned boat.

She heard Lesia moan, 'I'm so hungry. We've been here for almost two days. They left us water but nothing to eat.'

'Me too,' said Jane. 'I'm starving. I think it's the pregnancy. My appetite has really increased.'

She remembered one of her father's silly sayings, 'I'm so hungry I could eat a kid with measles.' He had meant it to be funny but it had always made Jane feel sick.

Agnieska turned to Jane.

'You're pregnant?'

Jane smiled broadly. 'Yes. I've just found out.'

'Patrick?'

'Of course.'

'Congratulations.'

Just at that moment the phone in her pocket rang. She lifted out the phone and put it to her ear.

'Hi. Dawn here. We've got the bastards. Well, two of them. Jack and Patrick have gone after the other one, in Patrick's car. Tell Lesia that Darren has been a real hero. It's safe for you to leave the boat now. A car will collect you and take you to that pub in the village. I'll let Jack and Patrick know where you are and I'll meet you there when I've finished here. OK?'

Agnieska announced the good news to the others. When Lesia heard the news about Darren she burst into tears. Then she began to feel dizzy and sank onto one of the beds. Jane hurried over and cradled Lesia's head in her lap. She really is just a kid, Agnieska thought.

'It's OK. We'll have you out of here soon.'

And in fact, at that moment, they heard a car pull up beside the boat.

Agnieska put down her knife and picked up the key. She opened the door. A man walked down the steps, but it was not a policemen. The man was quite elderly, very smartly dressed and he had a gun in his hand.

Agnieska grabbed for the knife but the man turned the gun on her, saying, 'Naughty, naughty...Put it on the floor. Now come along you lot. I need you for my protection.'

Jane spoke up. 'This girl is feeling faint. She hasn't eaten for two days.'

'Well there's plenty of food where we're going. Just get her to my car.'

Lesia managed to stand and supported by Jane and Agnieska she climbed the steps, got off the boat and into the man's car. She sniffed and frowned, saying, 'I've been in this car before.'

The man gave her a quizzical look but said nothing.

Agnieska tried to text Dawn without the man noticing. But he did and asked her to hand over the phone. Then he asked, 'Can you drive?'

'Of course.'

'Right. You drive. I'll sit in the passenger seat so I can keep an eye on you all. Follow my directions. It's not very far.'

They all got in the car. Agnieska was thinking how she might cause a slight accident and take over the car but the risk was too great with Jane and Lesia in the back seat.

'Do a three-point turn and go back to the road. Then turn left.'

Agnieska manoeuvred the car skilfully around the little canalside wharfage and drove towards the main road. She had decided that this was the man that Jack and Patrick were chasing but they had not guessed he would turn off the road so soon. They were probably well on their way to Whitchurch by now. There was just a chance that they would realise he wasn't going that way, and they would meet them coming back. If so she could flash the lights. She checked the way she would do this and drove as slowly as she could, her ankle hurting as she pressed the accelerator.

'Put your bloody foot down, woman. I want to be off the road when your friends decide to come back.'

After a mile further on he suddenly announced, 'Take the next right,' and they turned into a drive leading to a substantial house.

'Drive round the back. We'll be out of sight from the road.'

There were other cars in the driveway but they went past these, following a gravelled track between the house and several outbuildings.

'Park here. You two get out of the car first. Put your hands on the roof of the car and wait for me.'

It was obvious that Jane and Lesia were too scared to disobey and Lesia was still rather wobbly from lack of food.

'Now you!'

Agnieska thought for a moment of making a dash for the trees that surrounded the house, but with her ankle still so painful she would never make it.

The man with the gun ushered them before him into the house.

'The kitchen's that way.' He pointed down a corridor on the left.

The kitchen was large, very modern and well equipped.

'There's no one here to disturb us. My housekeeper won't be around till tomorrow. There are cereals in that cupboard and milk in the fridge. When you've chosen something to eat I want you to sit at this table and wait.'

'What for?' asked Agnieska.

'The arrival of the cavalry. If they agree to my terms you will be freed. If not...'

Lesia and Jane chose cereals from an extravagant range, poured in milk and sat at the table. Lesia was trembling as she spooned in mouthfuls of cereal. Jane suddenly felt nauseous and could not eat.

Agnieska lifted her swollen ankle on to a kitchen stool and asked calmly, 'So you're prepared to kill all of us to get free.'

'Well, I have no intention of going to prison at my age. Perhaps the police will be sensible. You see I have sensed them closing in for some time. First the West Midlands Drug Squad began to sniff around. Then I had a visit from that DI and his butch sidekick, so I prepared a little something earlier. You see I was in the army as a young man. Bomb making was my speciality.'

He took what looked like a small gas cylinder from a briefcase and attached the two wires leading from it to an electric socket, and fiddled with a dial on the top. Then he lifted his head to listen. 'Ah, I think that's them now.'

Several police sirens wailed as a row of cars entered the drive and pulled up with a screech of tyres on the gravel. The women started to move to the windows but the man waved his gun and ordered them back to the table. The doorbell rang and when it wasn't answered Dundee peered through the kitchen window. When he saw the man with the gun and his hostages sitting at the table he pulled back quickly. There was a pause then the man's phone rang. He laid it on the table and pressed loudspeaker, so that the women could hear.

174

'Preston! This is Detective Inspector Dundee. Your house is surrounded. You must put down your gun and let the women go.'

'I have no intention of harming these women so long as you do what I say. If you let me go for half an hour and don't enter this room, the explosive device I have fixed up will not go off. After that you are free to come in and release the women. If however you try to enter the room or the women try to leave before that time the device will explode. And if I see any sign of police activity as I drive away I shall set off the device with my mobile phone. Do you understand?'

'I understand that you are an evil man, Preston, and that you have been running a criminal organisation for some time. But...'

'But?'

'But I will abide by your conditions. You are free to leave.'

'Very well. I am going to set the device now. The timer will begin fifteen seconds after I leave the room. Synchronise watches at 18.20 hours.'

'Time set.'

Preston hurried over to the device, with his gun still in his hand. But he was in such a hurry he did not notice Agnieska's leg stuck out from beneath the table. He went flying and as he fell the gun he was holding caught the edge of the table. There was tremendous explosion but it was only his gun which had turned to face him as he fell. Preston dropped to the ground and did not move. Agnieska rubbed her ankle which had been badly hurt in her ruse. Then she hobbled over, turned off the power, and spoke into the phone still lying on the desk.

'It's OK. The device is disabled and I think Preston is dead.' Meanwhile Jane had gone to check on Preston and Lesia moved towards the gun, but then a loud voice spoke as Dundee and Eccles entered to room.

'Don't touch that. It's evidence.'

Eccles went over, checked that the safety catch was back on and dropped the gun into a plastic bag.

As more people came into the room the three women came together in a mammoth hug. Lesia laughed nervously.

'At least I'm not hungry any more.'

There was the sound of an altercation outside the kitchen door.

Dundee shouted, 'You can come in but don't touch anything.'

Patrick and Darren entered. Patrick went straight to Jane, a look of great concern on his face. Putting his arms around her he whispered, 'Are you all right? We heard the gun. I was terrified.'

'Just very tired,' she said as she nestled into his shoulder.

Darren had hesitated in front of Lesia, but she smiled and ran into his arms.

FORTY-THREE

Back in his office Dundee placed the two guns, still in their plastic bags, on his desk and examined them. One of the guns had been taken from Piggy and the other from Preston. He shook his head. Neither of the guns had the size and shape of butt to make that hole in the victim's head. So whose gun had killed Bernard Talbot and where was it now?

Forensics soon established that Preston's gun had been handled by no one but himself and that his death was accidental. After all, the man was quite elderly and adrenaline was obviously pouring through his veins, as he tried to organise his escape, so no wonder he had lost his footing. Neither Lesia nor Jane had seen Agnieska's outstretched foot and she decided not to complicate the issue.

Now that Preston was dead, his two accomplices in police custody and everyone was safe, it was time to recover those stolen cars. Working on the basis that the crooks had taken about an hour to remove three of the cars to their new hiding place and return to Moss Farm, a circle was drawn on the map with a circumference showing the most likely distance travelled. The area was carefully investigated for likely farm buildings or other hiding places and soon the cars were discovered in a barn left empty when a dairy farm had ceased to operate in the hills between Ruthin and Mold.

The stolen cars would need to be forensically examined before they could be returned to their owners, but there would be some telephone messages going out soon that would be joyfully received. It was decided that Patrick's Porsche was so thoroughly contaminated by Dundee and himself that there was no point in giving it any attention so he was able to drive it away.

FORTY-FOUR

Paul arranged to meet David at the lakeside café in Ellesmere during his lunch hour. This was on the opposite side of the town from the school and any kids sneaking out at lunchtime would get no further than the chippy or the burger place in the town centre.

Paul had told David that he wanted to discuss his return to school, but of course he had other, much more important things to ask. He arrived early, bought a soft drink and sat waiting at a table near the window overlooking the lake. The place was quiet at this time of year. Soon the herons would be nesting in the trees across on the island and dozens of visitors would be looking at the screens where the CCTV cameras showed heron mating rituals and breeding practices. Dad would have loved all that. Whatever had been going on in his life recently, which had probably led to his death, he had always been interested in wildlife. And Paul had to agree that this was a beautiful place, with the sun flashing on the rippling water and the geese, ducks and swans gathered at the lake's edge.

He heard the sound of David's beat up Mini arriving in the car park and steeled himself for this difficult interview. When David walked in he had a pile of books under his arm, probably intending to help Paul catch up before he returned to school. He placed the books on the table and asked, 'Hi Paul. Have you ordered yet? What can I get you?'

To be honest Paul had no appetite, but David obviously wanted to treat him and of course this was his own lunch break so he would be hungry. Paul agreed to have a chicken salad, so David went off to order. When he returned he sat down opposite and said, quietly, 'That was a terrible thing to happen. How is your mother now? I wanted to phone, but it didn't seem like a good idea.'

'She's not very well. Almost a nervous breakdown, I think.'

'Oh God. I never thought...But I suppose that's to be expected, considering what has happened.'

'You should have phoned. She would have appreciated it.'

David's face reddened. Paul wasn't sure whether this was with shame or anger.

'It was difficult. I didn't want to get mixed up in this. My wife...'

'I thought you and Mum were in love.'

'Good gracious no. We were just good friends. We had a lot in common. You know, art and books and theatre and the cinema. Whereas my wife...It was obvious that your mum and dad were not getting on. She needed someone to talk to.'

'Where did you talk to her?'

He reddened even more. 'What business of yours...'

At that moment the waitress came to their table and placed the food in front of them. Even when she had gone David didn't begin his meal. Eventually he seemed to calm down a little.

'OK. Yes I was fond of your mother and I know she liked me. Strangely enough this is one of the places we used to meet. And we spoke on the phone quite often. But it never went any further. I want you to believe that.'

To return to normality he began to pick at his food. Paul began his salad but it almost stuck in his throat. He decided push his luck.

'The police thought I'd killed my dad. They interviewed me at the police station.'

Paul could see he was shocked.

'What on earth made them think that you...?'

'I found this little hammer on the Moss. There was blood on the hammer head. Those detectives turned up just as I was inspecting it, so I threw it away. Stupid thing to do. So it had my

179

fingerprints on it. They took me to the station and gave me a grilling. Then suddenly I was released. Apparently the blood on the hammer wasn't my dad's.'

'That must have been horrible. What sort of hammer did you find?'

'Just a small one, but quite heavy, made of steel like that one you keep in your office; the one you use for breaking up rocks to get at the fossils. I know that fossil hunting is a hobby of yours. Oh and they found a bloodstained jacket like one that you wear sometimes. It was hidden under a bush on the Moss behind our cottages.'

'Well my little hammer is still in my office. And I certainly haven't lost a jacket. Anyway, you said the blood wasn't your dad's.'

With Paul's implied accusation dealt with he seemed to relax and began to eat his meal. Then he asked, 'Will you be coming back to school soon?'

'I hope not. Perhaps Mum and I will go back to Birmingham. I've always hated it here.'

'That's a shame. After all this is your GCSE year. You would do well, especially in art and English. I brought these books...'

'No way. There are too many bullies. And they know I'm gay.'

He paused, then changed the subject. 'Do you really think I should visit your mother?'

'I'm not sure now. She's really changed. I think she feels guilty about what's happened.'

'But surely she didn't have anything to do...'

'Oh no, I think it's because she'd stopped loving him.'

'Well look, would you tell her how sorry I am and if she wants...Anyway, I must get back. I'm really sorry. And you're sure about school?'

Paul nodded. David picked up the books and went to pay the bill. He gave a wave as he left the café. Paul no longer thought that he had had anything to do with his dad's murder. He was glad he'd cleared that up.

FORTY-FIVE

Lesia and Darren sat in an interview room at the police station. They had discovered that a restraining order against Darren had never officially been made. The threat to make one had just been Katie's fiancé Simon's way of frightening him off. Lesia had not made any charges against Darren and he had been commended for his help in catching those crooks.

'Lesia, can you ever forgive me?'

'I already have.'

'I can't believe how stupid I was. But I was desperate to see you, and I thought that order...'

'I know. I understand. It's OK now.'

'Are we really friends?'

'We're more than friends.'

Lesia leaned over and gave him a kiss on the cheek.

'The thought of that disgusting Piggy touching my chest still makes me feel sick.'

'I really enjoyed dumping him on the ground.'

Lesia chuckled, 'I'd love to have seen that.'

'What will you do now?'

'Well I've still got my job with the Wildlife Trust. They gave me time off when Mr Talbot was killed.'

'Perhaps you could have his job?'

'I wouldn't want that. I don't really want to go back to the Moss.'

'Yeah, I can understand that. What the hell was he up to? Talbot I mean. Was he dealing, like I thought?'

'Dundee says he was. By the way, they found your phone in that big guy's pocket. That was the proof. They'd have had enough evidence to arrest him, but of course he's dead. Anyway it's obvious that's how he could afford such a posh car.'

'Do you think that's why he was murdered? Was it a rival gang?'

'Seems that way. But it's not really our concern. I just feel such a fool to have liked him so much. Anyway, Darren, what are you going to do now? Will you go back to Birmingham?'

'No way. I want to stay near you. D'you reckon I could be a copper?'

Lesia burst out laughing. Darren was little offended. Then Lesia asked, 'Would you really want to do that?'

'Well I really like Dundee and Eccles. I really admire them. The way they caught those crooks. With my help of course. And I reckon I'd look good in uniform.'

'But don't you have to have qualifications? Like GCSEs?'

'I didn't do too bad. I ain't a brainbox like you, but I got five Cs.'

'You kept that quiet.'

'It didn't suit my image then. But I'm different now.'

Later that day Lesia was asked if she would like to come back to the wildlife centre. People had liked her happy smile when she had worked on the information desk and her knowledge had widened considerably since her time at the Moss. A new appointment would need to be made for Bernard's post but one of the wardens from another area was going to take over for a while. Lesia agreed to return to the Shrewsbury centre and she went back to Monkmoor to find out whether she was still able to stay with Kate.

Kate was delighted to see her and hugged her fiercely. She had heard some of Lesia's story from Radio Shropshire and had been worried sick. Lesia was not too sad to learn that Kate's engagement had been broken off. Apparently her fiancé had made some racist remark about blacks always being trouble and she had sent him packing with his ring following him through the door.

Lesia phoned her parents and gave them a much simplified and censored version of her adventures. They were so pleased to hear that she was safe and back in Shrewsbury and they arranged to come and visit her as soon as possible..

Kate decided that they should celebrate. She went out and bought a bottle of wine to share when their takeaway was delivered. They were just settling in front of the television to watch *Britain's Got Talent* (a guilty pleasure they also shared) when the doorbell rang. Kate was shocked to see Darren at the door and began to say, 'Should you...' but Lesia ran across saying, 'It's OK, Kate, we've sorted it out.' She dragged Darren into the room and gave him an enthusiastic embrace. He seemed embarrassed and muttered something about not wanting to intrude, but Kate poured him a glass of wine and Lesia put another plate to warm. Soon he relaxed and announced, 'I just came to say that I've taken a job as a barman at the theatre. It'll keep me going till I start college in September.'

Lesia leaned across and gave him a kiss on his lips. Hers tasted of curry.

DAY FIVE

FORTY-SIX

There was no point in Agnieska trying to continue her walk to Llangollen. Her ankle was still very painful and she had a lot to report when she returned to Drug Squad Headquarters. But the best news was still to come. When she got back to Birmingham she discovered that DI Prentiss had been suspended. Apparently he'd tried it on with another young recruit. Unlike Agnieska she'd had the sense to report him and incredibly she was believed. Of course Prentiss had tried to bluff it out, but this time the senior officer dealing with the complaint was female. It was likely that his suspension would eventually become dismissal.

Agnieska felt very relieved, though she did not want anyone, even DI Prentiss, to end his days in this way and lose his pension after so many years of service. But when she spoke to the other victim and discovered that Prentiss had actually pressed her against a wall and put his hand up her skirt she decided that he deserved everything he got.

The discovery of a load of cocaine in the boot of Preston's car was a real boost to the Drug Squad. Of course Preston was the brains behind the drugs trafficking and his death caused chaos among the gang. It wasn't long before they caught a couple of his dealers and learned from them that the trade in drugs had been developed using the canals as a route down from the north and that the Moss had become a centre for distribution.

One of the dealers told them that Bernard Talbot had returned to the Moss centre one night and saw two cars parked just inside the wood. Wondering what they were up to, he had crept up and watched a deal taking place. When he saw the amount of money involved he decided he wanted a piece of the action. When the client left, Talbot waylaid the dealer and threatened to report him to the police unless he received a cut.

If the drug dealers wanted to continue to use this very suitable spot they had to bring him in on the deals. Soon Bernard had developed his own circle of clients. It was easy money and he began to enjoy the high life, such as that expensive car, good clothes and gifts for his wife and son, way beyond the possibilities on his meagre income as a wildlife warden. But start playing with fire and sure enough you're likely to get burnt. Preston discovered what Talbot was up to and decided to get rid of the opposition.

Not only was Grabowski commended for her part in smashing the drug-trafficking gang but because of the changes following Prentiss's suspension she found herself promoted to detective sergeant. She felt rather guilty at so quickly reaching the same level as Eccles, who had been a detective sergeant for several years, but when Agnieska phoned her Dawn was quick with her congratulations and showed no sign at all of jealousy.

DI Prentis's fate, the result of another officer's complaint, changed the rest of the squad's attitude to Agnieska. They were all so busy tying up the loose ends of the investigation that teamwork was essential and the atmosphere in the squad was greatly improved.

FORTY-SEVEN

There were half a dozen detectives, ranging from Detective Superintendent Jane Rowley, a small woman with a sharp brain and a strong personality, to two young detective constables, gathered in the incident room. Dundee stood near a wall covered in mugshots and photos of locations and began his preamble.

'OK. The murder of Bernard Talbot. So where are we? Eccles?'

'Mr Talbot's body was found on the floor of his hallway in the early hours of February 20th by his son Paul. When Doctor Jones examined the body he reckoned that death had occurred about two hours previously. Mr Talbot had been dealt a blow to the back of his head with what we thought at first was a hammer, but now forensics think it was more likely to have been a pistol butt. The way he was lying and the lack of blood suggested that he had been killed elsewhere, brought to his house and dumped on the floor.'

One of the DCs asked, 'Did the lad, what's his name, Paul, touch the corpse?'

'He says not,' said Dundee. 'He came downstairs and saw his father lying there. At that moment he thought he heard someone leaving by the back door and hurried to look. But there was no one there. When he came back in he saw his mother coming downstairs and tried to stop her. He does seem particularly fond of his mother.'

'Almost unnaturally so,' added Dawn.

'Have the wife and son been cleared of any involvement?' The Detective Superintendent's voice was low and serious.

Dawn answered, 'We haven't found any real evidence to connect them to the crime. Doctor Jones suggested that the killer had to be tall and the wife is certainly not that. The son is tall and he was not getting on well with his father, but so far there is very little to suggest his involvement. We found him with a bloodstained hammer in his hands but the pathologist said that the hammer was the wrong shape to have killed the victim and the blood on it wasn't Talbot's.'

'So do we know whose blood it was?' asked one of the DCs.

Dundee said, 'Not yet. And we don't know why there was a blood stained hammer on the Moss where the lad apparently found it and picked it up. One of the many puzzles in this case.'

'So how's the wife managing now?'

'Not at all well. Her nerves are shot and she seems to be heading for a breakdown.'

'Guilt?' suggested the Detective Superintendent.

'Hmm,' muttered Dundee. 'We're going to interview her again. With a psychologist present. We'll see what comes out of that.'

Rowley asked, 'What about those two idiots you've just arrested? Could they have done it? After all they had a gun. And they could have carried the body between them.'

Dundee explained, 'They are both due to be questioned today. We'll see what we learn then. But their gun wasn't the right size to have caused the wound and there was no trace of blood on it. Personally I don't think they would actually shoot anybody. They used the gun to intimidate, rather than kill. But we'll see what the interviews bring up.'

Dawn said, 'But I wouldn't put it past Preston to shoot someone or hit them on the head. He was quite prepared to blow up his hostages in cold blood. He's obviously been running that gang for several years, while pretending to be a respectable solicitor. I gather a considerable haul of cocaine was found in the boot of his car.'

Mitsy Jenks, a young DC with a small, pretty face wanted to know about the drugs business. Dundee explained. 'The drugs squad have taken that on. Our colleague DS Grabowski, from

West Midlands Force, who by sheer coincidence was in the area, is leading the investigation, so I know it will be thorough. It does look as though Talbot got involved, so Preston had to warn him off. But whether he actually killed him we don't know.'

'And,' said the Detective Superintendent, who had been rather suspicious about the way Preston had died, 'it will be difficult to find that out now he's dead.'

Jim Hardy, the other DC, asked, 'What about those black kids? Were they involved with the drugs?'

Dawn answered, 'Not at all. The young guy, Darren, did a stupid thing. Simply to get a chance to show the girl how much he loved her. She has made no charges. They're an item now. And Darren showed great courage in helping us nab those culprits.'

'Another thing that puzzles me,' said Dundee, 'is that business with the money bag. I mean why dump several thousand in banknotes in a wet hole on the Moss. And what was a two-thousand-year-old corpse doing there in the first place?'

'Well at least we don't have to investigate that death,' said the Detective Superintendent. We'll leave that to the forensic archaeologists.'

Dundee suddenly became serious.

'OK. Actions. Eccles and I will be interviewing those miscreants beginning with the big guy.'

'I'd like to sit in on that if I may,' said the Detective Superintendent. Dundee wasn't too happy about that but he could hardly refuse.

Dundee turned to the detective constables.

'Jenks and Hardy. I'd like you to look into that bag. We never really discovered where it came from. Check with forensics and see if they have any further information about it. Then have another look at that hole in the Moss. I suppose we could call it a grave. See if you can find out how it was dug. We never found any tools. That might help us discover who made it and why.'

'Right, sir,' said Jenks, the pretty young constable. Eccles thought that Jack's eyes lingered rather too long on her. She knew what a sucker he was for attractive young women. And to be honest she was quite interested herself.

Hardy, her young male colleague was an unappetizing pudding of a man, and from what she had heard his brain was a bit stodgy as well. But Mitzy Jenks would keep him up to speed.

'That leaves you, Pringle.' Dundee addressed the Detective Sergeant lolling in his seat, hoping that he wasn't going to be given a job that required physical activity. He smiled when Dundee continued. 'I know your strength is in IT. I want to know everything you can find out about Preston. His life as a solicitor and as a crook. Anything you can turn up. Interests, relationships, whatever. Got it?'

'No problem, sir,' said Pringle as he rose slowly from his seat, moved to his desk and studied the screen of his beloved PC.

'Right, Eccles. The big man's in interview room three. Make sure there's an extra chair for the Superintendent. I'll be along in five minutes.'

'OK, boss,' said Eccles with a touch of sarcasm.

FORTY-EIGHT

Dundee turned on the video recording machine.

'Interview with Claude Claypole, timed 10.05a.m.'

Dundee found it hard not to snigger as he spoke the man's name. I mean how could that big slob slumped opposite him own the name of Claude. Eccles sat beside him at the table and the Detective Superintendent sat some distance away.

'Those present, Mr Claypole, Detective Chief Superintendent Rowley, Detective Sergeant Eccles, Detective Inspector Dundee and Mr Carl Chipway, Mr Claypole's legal adviser.'

Claypole scowled and half turned to his legal adviser as if to suggest that he was not even the person named.

Dundee continued, 'Mr Claypole, you are accused of multiple vehicle theft, the abduction and imprisonment of several adults and the use of a firearm to threaten them. What do you say?'

'I didn't fuckin' know those cars was pinched. I thought they belonged to the boss.'

'The boss being Mr Derek Preston.'

'Yea, that's 'im.'

'So you had no idea that the cars in the barn at Moss Farm were stolen?'

'I just knew he liked a pretty motor. He paid me to clean 'em up. And drive them to that new place.'

'But surely the paperwork?'

'I never saw no fuckin' paperwork. I told you I was employed as a mechanic and driver.'

'And what about the men and women on that boat?'

'Just fuckin' nosey buggers. I'd have let 'em go when we'd moved the motors.'

Eccles broke in, 'But you threatened them with a gun.'

'Naw, that were Piggy.'

'Come off it, Mr Claypole,' said Dundee. 'Your fingerprints were all over the gun.'

Mr Chipway lifted his hand to stop proceedings.

'Isn't it obvious, Detective Inspector,' Chipway addressed his remarks to Dundee, 'Preston had entrusted the gun to Mr Claypole as the older man, so he obviously handled it before handing it to his partner.'

Dundee asked, 'So why did they need a gun?'

Claypole answered, 'Preston asked us to look after his cars. They were fuckin' expensive. Wouldn't you want them looked after proper. He didn't want no nosey parkers knowing where they was.'

'That's because the cars were stolen and they were soon to be shipped abroad to new owners.'

'Like I said, I had no idea.'

Dundee asked, 'Did you know about the drugs?'

'I won't have nothing to do with drugs. I've seen what they can do. I've a nephew in one of them rehab places.'

'So you had nothing to do with Mr Bernard Talbot?'

'Whose he when he's at home?'

'A competitor of Mr Preston. Were you asked to warn him off?'

'What's he look like? This Talbot geezer?'

Eccles showed him a photograph of Bernard Talbot.

'Ah.'

'So you knew him?'

'So that was his name. Preston said this bloke had stole some money from him. We were to put the frighteners on him. We met the bloke on the Moss late one night. He had this money in a bag. We took the bag off him, tied him up and gagged him.

There weren't no one around at that time of night. Nasty sort of place that Moss is. So we dug this hole pretending we were going to bury him. While we were digging that geezer had managed to loosen the rope of his ankles. Suddenly he got up and ran. He was pretty fit. Too bloody fast for us, like. And it was dark anyway. Well at least we had the money. Piggy picked up the bag and went back to the hole. Then the moon came up and he saw this body at the bottom. He screamed and ran. Dropped the bag in the hole. I had no idea what had happened so I ran after him. We went to my house and downed a few pints. Then he told me about the body. Well neither of us wanted to go back there that night. We'd go back in the daylight, but when we did there was some blokes round that hole, lookin' in. So we scarpered.'

'So you didn't harm Mr Talbot in any way.'

'No, like I said, he run off. We couldn't catch him. Must have worked out I reckon. We told Preston we never saw him. He wasn't pleased would be an understatement.'

'Is there anything else you want to tell us, Mr Claypole?'

'Naw, that's about it.'

Dundee said, 'We shall want a statement, in writing.'

'I think,' said Chipway, 'that my client has been very helpful. Perhaps that will be taken into account when he goes to court.'

'Possibly,' said Dundee. 'Interview ended at 10.45am.'

This time DS Eccles led the interview.

'Matthew Piggott. Is that your name?'

The accused nodded.

'This interview is being recorded, so please speak aloud.'

'Yeah, that's my name.'

So that's why he's called Piggy, thought Dundee. Mind you he looks like a well fed piglet with dyspepsia.

'You are charged with multiple vehicle theft, the abduction and imprisonment of several people and of threatening them with a firearm. Do you have anything to say?'

Piggy looked at his lawyer, looked back at Eccles, smirked and said, 'No comment.'

'Mr Piggott, have you got a driving licence?'

Piggy was momentarily thrown by the change of direction. At last he smirked again and said, 'No comment.'

'We can find no record of you having such a licence. Yet you drove a very fast and expensive car to a new location. How do you explain that?'

'No fucking comment.'

'Very well. We'll move on. We have several witnesses who reported that you aimed a gun at them. That gun was later found to be loaded. Do you admit to handling such a weapon?'

'No comment.'

Eccles looked heavenward and sighed. What is the point? she thought.

Piggott's legal adviser whispered something to his client. After a pause the young lout said, 'OK so I had this gun. It was Claypole who give it me. Told me to keep 'em covered. Them nosey bastards.'

'Would you have fired the gun if Mr Claypole had ordered you to?'

'No comment.'

Eccles looked at Dundee, who shook his head. Eccles announced,

'Interview terminated at 11.30a.m.'

The two suspects were back in their cells. There was enough evidence to convict them both of several offences, and they would almost certainly receive custodial sentences, but had they killed Talbot?

'I reckon Claypole's story was largely accurate,' said Dundee. 'He's a crook all right, but I don't think he's a killer. I think we can call off the enquiry into the bag. We know what happened now.'

Eccles asked, 'What has Pringle discovered about Preston?'

Dundee picked up the folder Pringle had left on his desk and flicked through it.

'Apparently he was a genuine solicitor to begin with and quite a good one. But when his wife died three or four years ago he went off the rails. She had a large private income and he was expecting to benefit from her will, but he discovered she'd been cheating on him with some toy boy and her money was nearly all gone. So he decided to improve his income in other ways. First it was just at the office, overcharging and fiddling his expenses, then some alterations to wills. But then he was caught with his hand in the till in a bigger way and was given the push. No publicity, he was coming up to retirement anyway. But he got greedy. He found out about the drug racket using the canal which bordered his garden and got involved. The stolen cars business seems to have been a sideline, but lucrative never the less. That's how he got mixed up with some very unsavoury characters, like Claypole and Piggott.'

Jack closed the folder and placed it back on his desk, saying, 'Pringle's a bit of a couch potato, but put him in front of a PC and he comes up with the goods.'

Dawn nodded. 'Well, at least Preston's not our concern any more. Claypole's just stupid but Piggott's a nasty piece of work.

He's capable of anything if he was pushed. But somehow I don't think he killed Talbot.'

'So if neither of them killed him who the hell did?'

FORTY-NINE

By late afternoon DI Dundee had had enough of the Talbot case. It had been late night finishes for days. He hadn't had a chance to talk properly to Leanne since the miscarriage and the twins had almost forgotten what he looked like. They were still asleep when he left in the morning and back in bed before he got home. This wasn't fair on them or on him. He loved those kids. He'd promised to show Sean how to catch a rugby ball properly. The lad was growing fast and showing a definite physical aptitude. Karen was altogether more scholarly. Her school work was always meticulous, she was always curious and her lovely smile made her popular. Jack could hardly believe how well they'd settled into their new school, but apparently it was one of the best in the town.

When Jack got home there was still some light in the sky so he and Sean hurried to the park. He showed his son how to wait and watch as the ball came down and to hold it tight like a baby when it landed in his arms. At first Jack only sent it into the air from a short distance, but he gradually increased the distance until the ball was looping down to Sean from about twenty-five metres and he caught the ball more times than he dropped it. Jack was about to increase the distance again when he realised he could hardly see Sean at all.

'Come on, lad. It's getting dark. Let's get home.'

Sean held the ball tightly as they hurried across the road. He was past holding his father's hand but he walked close beside him feeling proud. When they went into the house, Leanne was in the kitchen preparing their favourite, spaghetti bolognese.

Karen was sitting at the table doing her homework. Jack looked over her shoulder at the page of neat, even handwriting, very different from his own scrawl. He put his hand on her shoulder and she looked up at her dad with that lovely smile. But before he could ask her about her work, Leanne called from the kitchen. 'Can you lay the table, Jack?'

The meal was hot and tasty. Soon they were all full of food and Jack and Leanne were finishing a glass or two of cheap red wine. If only, thought Jack as he filled the dishwasher, we could have more evenings like these. But that could only be achieved if he had an ordinary nine to five job. The trouble was that for all the long hours, the sudden dropping of plans so that he could follow up an enquiry, which irritated Leanne or disappointed the twins, he still loved his job. No day was quite the same as another. Yes, the paperwork was getting ridiculous, but when they finally cracked a case and the handcuffs were slipped over some villain's wrists it gave him a great sense of achievement.

But this latest case was getting to him. The more they learned what had happened the less they knew who had murdered Bernard Talbot. On reflection he was also worried about the way his friends had got involved in the case. They may have been shot or blown up. What the hell would he have felt then?

Jack took the kids to bed. Sean wasn't interested in bedtime stories any more. He liked to draw for a while. Cartoon characters. Jack could see a developing talent in these drawings. Miss Simkins at the school had commented on them as well. But tonight the drawing didn't last long. The lad was obviously tired and soon put his sketchbook and pencil on the bedside table and snuggled down under the duvet. Jack managed to sneak a kiss on his forehead before Sean noticed, and responded with a grunt.

Karen was reading when Jack looked in. It was *The BFG*, which she had read umpteen times before. Jack took over for a while. Karen liked that. She soon closed her eyes but when Jack stopped reading she opened them again.

'Go on, Daddy.'

So he went on reading. Next time her eyes closed, her breathing slowed as well, and she did not wake as Jack put the book back on the shelf, kissed his daughter and crept away.

Downstairs, Leanne was watching *EastEnders*. She had followed this soap for years. Jack knew better than to interrupt, so he simply sat beside her on the sofa and took her hand in his. He tried to follow the story but the characters seemed to spend most of the time either shouting at one another or sobbing. What a miserable lot, thought Jack. Then the familiar signature tune began. Leanne turned off the television and buried her head in Jack's chest. After a while Jack realised that she was crying.

'Hey, love, what's up?'

He lifted her tear stained face and kissed her gently.

'Oh, Jack, I know we didn't want that baby, but now it's gone, I feel lost.'

'You're probably just tired. That's such horrible thing to have to go through.'

'But suppose...'

'No, the baby wasn't meant to be. We have two lovely kids. We must be grateful and move on.'

Jack put his arm around Leanne's shoulder and drew her close. At that moment his phone rang. He looked at the caller's name, sighed, took his arm from around his wife and walked into the hall.

'Jack?'

'Yes?'

'Sorry to call you at home. Is it convenient to talk?'

'Not really. But knowing you, it's an idea you've had.'

'It is.'

There was a pause.

'Well go on.'

'Jack, you know that flower that Talbot was holding in his hand.'

'Yes.'

'Well I was wondering whether it wasn't just something he'd grabbed, but something he was trying to tell us.'

Jack was feeling irritable now. 'How can a flower tell us anything?'

'I don't know, but...did we ever identify the flower?'

'No. I didn't think it was important.'

'Do you think Lesia would know what it was?'

'She might. Look, can we leave this till tomorrow? I'm just talking to Leanne about what happened to her.'

'Oh God, Jack. I'm so sorry. I wouldn't have...'

'Look, we'll see what Lesia has to say tomorrow. OK?'

'Yes, Jack. Sorry.'

FIFTY

As the Porsche burbled its way back along the A5 towards Shrewsbury Patrick raised his voice to be heard above the engine.

'It's great to have the car back. Thirty years old and going like a bomb.'

Jane shouted back, 'I'd rather not talk about bombs.'

'Oh, sorry. That was silly of me. Anyway, it's all over now.'

'Yes, and I think I've seen enough of that Moss to last me a lifetime.'

'But it was good to see Jack and Dawn again, wasn't it.'

'And Agnieska too.'

'That was bad news about Leanne.'

'Well at least you're all right, in spite of everything.'

'Yes, never felt better.'

'Did you manage to get through to Tony to give him your news?'

'No, Mrs Taylor said he wasn't back yet, from wherever he's gone. She said she thought he might phone them this evening.'

'Does he have your number?'

'Oh yes. He often rings me. That's why I was so surprised to hear he'd gone away without telling me.'

They were approaching Shrewsbury and would soon have to decide whether to turn into the town or continue along the bypass.

'Shall we turn off here? Have a look round.'

'No, let's go on. I know Shrewsbury pretty well. It's where Mum and I used to go for posh shopping. You know, weddings, christenings, special parties. Unless you want to go?'

Patrick said, 'Not really. I'd rather get back to Bridgeport. Have another look at that wonderful steam railway.'

'That's fine by me,' she answered. 'If we stayed overnight I could visit Mum's grave tomorrow. I've been feeling rather guilty about neglecting it.'

They reached the roundabout where they would have turned left had they been going into Shrewsbury. Instead Patrick stayed on the dual carriageway and put his foot down.

'Where shall we stay?' he asked. We can't really expect Moira to put us up.'

'Of course if I hadn't sold Dad's house...'

'You wouldn't really have wanted to stay there?'

'No, you're right. Too many bad memories. Especially that poor girl whose body was found in my father's grave.'

'Indeed. Well we'd better find a hotel.'

FIFTY-ONE

When they entered the wildlife centre DI Dundee spotted Lesia already behind the desk, speaking to a member of the public and showing them a leaflet. That person moved away and Lesia smiled at her new friends and greeted them in a very professional manner.

'Good morning. How can I help you?'

'You look much happier now,' said Dawn.

'I love it here,' said Lesia.

'How's Darren?' asked Dundee.

'Oh no, he hasn't done something stupid, has he?'

'Not as far as we know. Anyway, it's your expert advice we need.'

'Oh.'

When Mr Talbot's body was found...'

Lesia's smile faded.

'A plant was found clutched in his hand.'

Dawn continued, 'We wondered if you might be able to identify it?'

She unwrapped a tissue and laid the plant, now rather withered, on the information desk.

Lesia studied it for a moment.

'Wow, that's quite a rarity. *Menyanthes trifoliata*. Difficult to spot at this time of the year. And it only grows in one part of the Moss. When it flowers it's quite beautiful.'

'Would you be able to show us where that plant grows?' asked Eccles.

'Oh yes.'

'I'll have a word with your boss,' said Dundee. 'Then you can come with us. If you don't mind?'

'If it helps in any way to find Bernard's killer I'd be glad to. I mean, I don't hate the Moss, though I wouldn't want to work there again. Nature is wonderful. It's just people who spoil things.'

Dawn nodded. Soon they were all on the way to the Moss.

They parked near the Moss centre where the new warden was preparing for the first group since the murder to visit next day. From there Lesia led them across the Moss, past the grave where the ancient corpse had been unwittingly revealed by the nefarious activities of Claypole and Piggott. From there they walked across the open Moss, a chill wind causing them to turn up their coat collars despite the sunshine sparkling on the ditches on either side of the track. Soon the detectives glimpsed the buildings of Moss Farm among the leafless trees ahead. But Lesia took another path to the left.

Suddenly Dundee knew exactly where they were. The row of cottages came into view beyond the copse. In fact they were immediately behind the cottage of that Briggs chap, with the copse between. Lesia told them to tread carefully now or they might destroy the few specimens of that rare plant. Eccles asked Dundee, 'Wasn't this where that bloodstained jacket was found?'

'Yes. Just over there.'

'And didn't Briggs tell us he might have seen somebody out here that morning?'

'Hmm,' muttered Dundee.

Lesia pointed at a small group of plants on the edge of the path.

'There, look. Do you see them? Just one little patch down there.'

Dundee bent to pick one. Lesia stopped him.

'No, don't pick one. They're too rare. I have my camera here. It has a zoom lens.'

She took a few shots then showed them the image on the screen. They could see at once that it was the same sort of plant that Talbot had been holding.

'So,' said DI Dundee, 'he wanted to show us where he had been attacked. He knew how rare these plants were and grabbed one hoping that someone would recognise it. Which, thank goodness, our young expert was able to do.'

Not exactly a blush, but a happy flush came to Lesia's brown cheeks.

Dundee went on, 'Right we need SOCO over here pronto. I doubt there'll be any blood traces, after all the rain we've had, but I reckon we might find the murder weapon somewhere near here.'

'If it was the butt of a pistol, as forensics suggested,' said Eccles, 'would someone throw a gun away?'

'Perhaps not. But we're not entirely sure it was a gun.'

Lesia suddenly pointed to a bush a few feet away where her sharp young eyes had caught sight of something.

'What's that over there?'

It was a few moments before the detectives could see what she was pointing at.

Eccles asked, 'Shall we leave it for SOCO?'

'No way,' exclaimed Dundee. He pulled some rubber gloves out of his pocket, put them on, and thrust his hands into the bush. Holding it by the tip of the handle he drew out a golf club, beginning to rust slightly but with a darker stain on the business end.

'Well, well. Look at that.'

'It's a five iron,' said Eccles.

'How on earth do you know that?'

'I used to play golf with Trish. I was quite good.'

'Another of your many talents.'

Lesia had gone very quiet. Then she said, 'That stain? Is it blood?'

'I think it probably is,' said Dundee.

FIFTY-TWO

Paul had been really worried about his mum for quite a while. She hardly ever left her room. She looked dreadful. She hadn't washed her hair for ages. It just hung in limp clumps and he wasn't sure she had even washed herself properly. She didn't smell too good. Her face was very pale and her hands trembled all the time. Sometimes she didn't even seem to know he was there, then she'd suddenly grab him and sob, sob, sob. She needed help, but he didn't know who to ask.

She was taken back to the police station and questioned again. When she came home she was in a terrible state. Paul made her some tea but she just sat there until it went cold, then she went up to her room. He thought he should make her something to eat. He couldn't remember the last time he'd seen her eat anything. She used to love poached egg on toast, and that was something he could cook. When he looked in the cupboard there was only one egg and half a loaf beginning to go stale, but he decided it would still make good toast. He was going to have to go shopping next day.

Paul took the egg on toast to her room. When he knocked on the door she didn't answer. He took the food in. God, the room stank. The window hadn't been opened for ages. He lifted the sash just a fraction. When he approached the bed she moaned slightly and muttered, 'Go away.' So he left her to go back to sleep. He knew she hadn't been sleeping very well. Sometimes she would get up in the night and walk around the house. He had heard her talking to herself. Perhaps if she had a good night's sleep she'd be better in the morning.

Paul suddenly realised how hungry he was and tucked in to the egg on toast. He looked in the cupboard again and began to make a list of what they needed. Perhaps his mum would be able to drive them into Ellesmere tomorrow and they could go to

Tesco's. Paul made another piece of toast, scraped the last jam from a jar and wolfed that down as well.

He turned on the television and sat on the settee. He had absolutely no idea what he watched. Soon he was fast asleep. When he woke again it was late. He turned off the telly and went up to bed. He listened at Mum's door but she seemed to be sleeping properly so he didn't disturb her.

Next morning when Paul went into her room he knew at once that something was wrong. She was lying in the bed, very still, apparently asleep, but her face was as white as a sheet. He tried to find a pulse but there didn't seem to be one, then...yes, there it was, but very faint. He could have screamed with relief.

Then he noticed the box on the bedside table. Her sleeping tablets. He looked in the box but it was empty. He knew immediately that he had to wake her. He shook her, gently at first, then more vigorously. She gave a slight moan, then slipped back into unconsciousness. He phoned for an ambulance but thought it was probably too late. While he waited he searched the room for a note but she hadn't even bothered to leave one. He thought his mother had really loved him. He had certainly loved her.

Paul tried shaking her again. Her eyes briefly fluttered open and he burst into tears. Soon he heard a siren and knew that the ambulance had arrived. He went down to let the paramedics in. They were calm and efficient. One of them felt for a pulse, just as he had done, then gave Paul a nod and a smile. They put his mother on a stretcher, with straps to stop her falling off, carried her downstairs and into the ambulance. Paul was sweating with worry and with trying to keep her awake, but when he went outside he realised how cold it was and went back for a coat. Another paramedic shouted at him. 'Come on, lad. There's no time to lose.'

In the ambulance he tried to hold his mum's hand but it was so limp she might have been dead. When they reached the Royal Shrewsbury Paul was left in a waiting room while his mum was dealt with. He still couldn't believe she had done such a selfish thing. He would have been an orphan. What on earth would have happened to him?

A large, middle aged woman in messy clothes and lots of scarves introduced herself as Brenda, a social worker. She gave him a cup of tea from a machine and asked him all sorts of questions about himself and his mum. Of course she had heard about the murder. Paul didn't really want to talk. He suddenly felt very tired. He lay back in the comfortable chair and drifted off to sleep. He didn't know how long he had slept for, but when he woke the social worker had gone and there was a nurse in the room. She spoke very gently.

'Paul. Your mother is going to be fine.'

Tears came again, then he asked, 'Can I go and see her?'

'You can look in but you mustn't disturb her. They had to pump out her stomach, so she's very tired. Perhaps tomorrow...'

They had given her a private room. She was asleep, but it was a proper sleep this time. Paul could see her chest going up and down with her breathing. After a few moments the nurse ushered him away and took him back to the waiting room. When he opened the door he saw the detectives sitting inside. He called out angrily.

'You did this!'

The woman detective said, 'We're really sorry about your mum, Paul. We've come to take you home.'

'No way, I'm never going back there.'

Eventually he agreed to go back with them to collect some of his things, then they took him to a large house in Shrewsbury, where a plump, grey haired woman called Mrs Bray showed him a nice room, and said he could stay there until his mother had recovered. Apparently, Brenda, the social worker had arranged this. Mrs Bray didn't ask too many questions, she was used to dealing with troubled youngsters. He supposed that's what the police thought he was.

Mrs Bray told him that her own children were grown up and had left home long ago, so she looked after young ones who needed a temporary place to live. The detectives left and the woman gave him the first proper meal he had eaten for days.

Next day, after a large fried breakfast, Mrs Bray, who wanted him to call her Maureen, put him in her little car and took him back to the hospital and waited while he visited Mum.

She was awake, but looked very pale. There was a slight sparkle in her eyes and Paul knew that she was going to be OK. When she saw him she smiled and opened her arms, and tried to hug him, but she was too weak. He sat on her bed.

'Oh, Paul,' she said, 'I am so sorry. What I did was very wrong. Can you ever forgive me?'

Paul just nodded and kissed her cheek.

'They say you saved my life.'

He changed the subject.

'Those detectives still haven't caught the murderer. They told me they had some suspects but nothing could be proved.'

'I don't really care any more. Bernard is dead. We must make a new life for ourselves.'

'Mum, I never want to go back there.'

'That's all right, Paul. Neither do I.'

They hugged again and this time she seemed to have recovered some of her strength. They talked about going back to Birmingham. She suggested that he should go back to his old school. Perhaps he would have time to catch up before his

GCSEs. Apparently the house on the Moss belonged to the Wildlife Trust, so they could leave anytime.

FIFTY-THREE

Dundee and Eccles had been horrified to hear about Mrs Talbot's attempted suicide. They had taken the boy to stay with a woman the police had used before when there were no relatives to look after a child involved in a case. Obviously they wondered whether it was guilt that had led Mrs Talbot to try to try to take her own life. But it was impossible to imagine that she went out at night onto the Moss alone, hit her husband on the head with a golf club, carried him home, dumped him on the floor and calmly went back to bed. Had she been helped? By her son? By someone else? A lover perhaps? That chap Hurst? No, the timing was all wrong.

The boy was distraught, of course. Even Eccles had begun to feel sorry for him. She wondered whether she and Dundee had been the ones responsible for the boy's mother's action. Had they tipped her over the edge? After looking at the matter again she, and Dundee, decided that neither the mother or her son or both had done the deed. No, they were looking for a strong, golf playing, male who held a terrible grudge against Bernard Talbot. 'Or someone with an accomplice,' said Dundee.

'You mean Claypole or Piggott?

'Can you imagine any respectable golf club allowing those monsters to join?'

Forensics soon confirmed that the blood on the golf club came from Bernard Talbot. It had been protected from the weather by that thick bush. The SOCOs had not seen the club deep in the bush but Lesia's clear young eyes had spotted it. The pathologist showed a perfect match between the wound on his skull and the blade of the club. But there were no fingerprints on the shaft. It had been wiped.

Careful examination of the area produced no more blood, which had probably been washed away, but there were definite signs of a scuffle where the turf had been flattened. So now the detectives knew where the murder had taken place, but of course two important questions remained: who was the murderer and how, if he or she was alone, did they move the body from that place to the hallway of the Talbot home without dragging it along the floor and leaving tell-tale signs.

So it was back to square one. DI Dundee thought they should begin again at Lilac Cottage.

When they reached the cottages next to the Moss there was an eerie silence. No sign of life anywhere, except a light upstairs in Tom Perry's house. He was probably dealing with his poorly wife. The car was not outside the young foreign couple's home, so they were at work. Briggs was most likely walking around somewhere.

Lilac Cottage already felt abandoned. Of course Julie Talbot was recovering in hospital and the boy was with Mrs Bray in Shrewsbury.

These were cheaply built rural workers cottages, without things like damp courses, and as the detectives opened the door they felt dampness already permeating the walls, now that the house was unheated. It had looked cosy when the detectives had first visited, even with a body lying in the hallway, but now it smelt damp and distinctly unwelcoming. The place had seen a murder and an attempted suicide within a few days. They knew that SOCO had examined the place thoroughly but they wanted to reacquaint themselves with the events of the morning of that murder.

Dundee began, 'We now know that the body was dumped here in the hallway so I reckon it was brought in through the front door which was, according to Briggs, unlocked. The body was put down with the head facing the door to make us think that the victim was trying to escape that way just before he was killed.'

Eccles took up the tale. 'But we are sure now that the murder had taken place earlier and not in here. When the boy came downstairs the body had been there for some time. Something caused him to come down just at that moment?'

'So the figure Briggs thought he saw was probably nothing to do with the murder.'

'Well, we'll go and see him again. In case he's remembered anything else.'

'Is it worth talking to Tom Perry again?'

'We'll go and speak to him when we've finished with Briggs.'

They found Briggs in his back garden pushing a heavy wheelbarrow with its wheel covered by a rubber tyre. In the wheelbarrow was a large bag of peat. Eccles watched in awe as the man lifted out the heavy bag and placed it on the ground. She wondered if the compost was peat free, then another thought crossed her mind, but disappeared as the man turned to them with an angry look.

'That poor young woman. It's your fault. You harassed her until she tried to take her own life. And after all she'd suffered at the hands of that bastard husband.'

'Can we have a quick word?'

'Yes, I suppose. Let's go inside.'

'I'm sorry about Mrs Talbot,' said Dundee. 'We both are.'

'Such a sweet little thing,' said Briggs as they entered the house by the back door. Inside, he asked, 'Well, what is it?'

'On the morning of the murder you said you thought you saw someone lurking about at the back of the house. Can you tell us about that again?'

'Yes. I was just coming back from a stroll along the lane. My feet were muddy so I came round the back to take off my boots. As I turned to scrape off the mud by the door I thought I saw someone slipping into the copse. I couldn't make out who it was and they disappeared pretty quickly. Then poor Julie began to scream and I went into their cottage.'

'Which way did that person go?' asked Dundee.

'If you follow me I can show you exactly.'

The detectives were about to follow Briggs back outside when Dawn's phone rang. 'Eccles,' she announced, then to Briggs and Dundee, 'It's OK. I'll catch you up.'

The two men left. She quickly answered the query, something about working hours from someone in the salaries department, then went to follow the men. Between the living room and kitchen the stairs went up to the bedrooms. Under the stairs was a cupboard and the door had been left open. Eccles couldn't help glancing inside. She saw a set of golf clubs. Now she couldn't resist checking. It was a complete set: except for a missing five iron.

Eccles went into the garden and called to Dundee.

'Hurry up, Jack. They want us back at the station.'

'Right. Thanks for that, Mr Briggs. Nothing else you can tell me?'

'No. But I still partly blame you for that lovely young woman's attempt to kill herself.'

Eccles called impatiently, 'Come on, Jack.'

Back in the car, Dundee asked, 'So what's so important?'

Eccles put the car in gear and moved off.

'Nothing, except I think I know who killed Bernard Talbot.'

'You do? Well who?'

'You were just talking to him.'

Jack looked at his partner as if she was mad, then asked, 'And what brings you to that conclusion?'

'Two things. First there's a set of golf clubs in his house, missing a five iron. Secondly he has a wheelbarrow.'

'What the hell has a wheelbarrow got to do with it? Hey look out!'

Dawn's excitement was causing her to drive rather erratically. Now they were away from the cottages she could stop. She found a lay-by and pulled in. Jack knew that if Eccles had an idea it was usually worth listening to.

'OK. Convince me.'

'Look. Briggs had a real thing about little Mrs Talbot. And he hated her husband. He knew how the man was treating his wife.'

'Go on.'

'Did you see the way he lifted that big bag of peat out of his wheelbarrow? He may be getting on but he's still a strong man. And if you wanted to move a body to another place, what would you use?'

Jack was beginning to understand and smiled. 'A bloody wheelbarrow. Hey, this is making sense!'

'And that set of clubs, without a five iron, is the clincher. Look. Just phone the station and ask them what they have on Roland Briggs.'

The information came back swiftly. Briggs had indeed been in the forces, as a commando in the Falklands and Northern Ireland. He had twice been awarded medals for bravery. Then he was dismissed for assaulting an officer, almost fatally. He also came under suspicion by the police when his wife died after falling down the stairs and injuring her head. Apparently she had fallen onto a loose stair rod and caused a nasty wound to the back of her head. But nothing could be proved and the man had such a good reputation locally as a magistrate that no further investigation had taken place.

'Right, let's call for backup. He must be arrested and brought in for questioning.'

'Oh, just one more thing. He has a shotgun. Properly licensed.'

'So we may need an armed unit.'

'OK, let's all meet at the Moss centre. Briggs doesn't know he's a suspect, so we may surprise him.'

It took almost an hour to get the whole team assembled, partly because their superiors were unconvinced at first, but eventually the group met at the Moss centre, with most wearing bulletproof vests and a couple of officers who were armed, then they all moved towards Briggs' cottage. There was no sign of him outside. Dundee began to wonder if he'd put two and two together and realised they were on to him and left in a hurry. The rest of the team took up their positions and DI Dundee walked towards the front door. Suddenly Briggs shouted, 'Stop right there, Dundee, or I'll blow a fucking hole in your head.'

Jack saw Briggs leaning out of an upstairs window, with a shotgun in his hands.

'It's no use, Briggs. The house is surrounded. I've come to arrest you for the murder of Bernard Talbot.'

'I don't regret it for a moment. That jumped up pipsqueak telling me what I should do and shouldn't do, and beating his lovely wife. He got what he deserved.'

Well his confession had been heard by enough witnesses to make it stand. Now they had to get the man himself into custody.

'Put the gun down and come outside, Mr Briggs. You'll gain nothing by killing one of us.'

'Sorry, I've done with doing what I'm told. Had enough of that in the fucking army. I did my duty and what did I get? Not even a proper fucking pension.'

'I'm giving you five minutes. Then we're coming in.'

Briggs didn't reply. Dundee informed him as each minute passed.

'You have one minute left to put down your gun and come out.'

Suddenly there was an explosion inside the house and a curl of smoke wafted through the open window. Then there was just a stunned silence, except for rooks calling in panic as they rose from the trees. The armed police went into the cottage to check, before telling the detectives it was safe to enter. They found Briggs in the bedroom, sitting with his back against the wall, the shotgun held between his legs, the barrel in his mouth and his head half blown away.

Jack Dundee began to wonder if these cottages were cursed. A murder, an attempted suicide and a proper suicide in less than week! Christ, what a mess.

FIFTY-FOUR

With the murder solved and the stolen cars returned to their owners DI Jack Dundee was able to relax for a while. He decided to take the few days' leave owing to him. If anything serious cropped up he was sure that DS Eccles could cope. She had really been the one who had solved the murder case. Dawn was a good detective and great partner. Leanne had not yet returned to work after the miscarriage and it was the twins' half-term holiday. Spring had come early this year. The sun was already giving out some warmth, there were buds beginning to appear on the trees, there were clumps of snowdrops in the hedgerows and daffodils were opening everywhere. The kids were delighted to have their dad at home. It was just Leanne who seemed unable to share the good mood.

Since losing the baby she had been quite depressed. Obviously it had been an unpleasant experience, painful and disturbing, but it was more than that, she felt bereft. Perhaps she had begun to accept the existence of the child which had never been born and now there was just this emptiness. It would have changed their lives, and caused all sorts of problems, but…

Jack decided that they all needed a day out. He wanted to explore some of the countryside near Shrewsbury. North? No, that would remind him too keenly of recent events in that direction, so they would go south. They needn't go far. One of his colleagues had told him about Lyth Hill, which was near the village of Bayston Hill, where she lived just three miles out of Shrewsbury.

'There's a path, right across the top. You can park your car and have a really good walk. Mary Webb, the famous Shropshire writer, used to have a cottage up there. The views are fantastic.'

Jack had never heard of Mary Webb, but then he was not an avid reader. Leanne liked romantic novels but they didn't interest him. And he found crime novels completely unbelievable.

So he suggested they go to Lyth Hill, and afterwards they could visit McDonald's at Moele Brace, in the valley below. The twins cheered, but whether that was for the walk or the treat which was to follow he wasn't sure.

Leanne wasn't convinced she wanted the walk or the treat, but she didn't want to be a drudge, so after breakfast they piled into the car and set off. Their journey began along Gains Park Way which took them onto the B4386 past the Royal Shrewsbury Hospital, where poor Julie Talbot was still recovering from her attempt to end her life. Jack thought that had been a really selfish act, when she had a teenage son to consider. In fact it was her son's prompt action that had saved her life. What had driven her to take such drastic action he would never understand, but then he had never been put in her position, with a husband murdered in her own home and suspicion falling on her. Well, at least any suspicion had been removed and the real murderer found. Perhaps now she would think about her son and make a new start, possibly back in Birmingham, where the boy certainly wanted to be.

They turned on to what Jack had been told was the old A5 but thankfully no longer had to carry that weight of traffic now the bypass had been built in fields outside the town. They passed the Meole Brace retail park on their left and Sean called out, 'Hey look. There's McDonald's. Can we go now?' But his sister told him, rather priggishly, that they had to have a good walk first, to which he muttered, 'S'ppose.'

They negotiated the big roundabout where they crossed the new bypass and made their way up the village of Bayston Hill. After a sharp right turn they continued along a road lined at first with pleasant suburban houses, until these thinned out and the road became steeper and narrower and ended at last in a rather bumpy, muddy car park, where a few cars had already released their occupants onto the hill.

Leanne stood for a moment, looking at the view, which stretched for miles across a wide valley towards blue-green hills in every direction. 'Wow!' she said, smiling for the first time in ages. Jack joined her, putting his arm around her waist, and saying, 'Not bad, eh.'

The twins had already climbed the stile leading to the footpath and were running delightedly across an open field, calling and whooping at their freedom. But by the time they had walked across the first long field, they had returned to their parents and were walking more steadily beside them.

They were not alone. There were many other walkers going the same way or coming back in the opposite direction, and most of them were accompanied by dogs, on leads or running free. There were large dogs, small dogs and middle sized dogs, of all breeds and mixtures. One ugly little creature bounded over and asked to be petted. Jack saw that smile again on Leanne's face as she tickled the little dog behind the ears, until it was called away by its owners.

They went through another gate and onto a rocky headland where they studied a three dimensional map which had been set up on a kind of table. This showed the names of the hills facing them, from Cannock Chase on the far left, then the Wrekin and the other hills that seemed to float across the flat land, like a fleet of upturned galleons. Directly in front of them was the Long Mynd and slightly further away the Stiperstones rose like a spiny dinosaur and finally there was Pontesbury Hill on the far right. All these were places to be visited as the kids got older and were able to walk further. Then a thought came to Jack that had the child lived they would have had to wait quite a few more years before they were able to do that. But he did not speak his thought aloud.

Below them in the valley there were neat fields, some with cows or sheep in them, having been released from their winter quarters. Dotted among the fields were farm buildings or single cottages, like a child's picture book of the countryside.

As he stood looking out at that sublime landscape Dundee thought about his daily battle with crime. It seemed to be getting worse each day and under resourced as they undoubtedly were the task became more difficult. Look at all the evil he had dealt with recently. There was Preston who had taken to crime as a kind of revenge, without considering the harm his drugs were doing to so many, especially young people. Then there were those idiots, Claypole and Piggott. They probably came from poor homes, starved of parental love and guidance, so they got involved in petty crime as youngsters, which then became less petty and more harmful as they grew older. And what about Bernard Taylor, who was a lover of nature and a talented teacher, but greed had caused him to go off the rails. He got his comeuppance at the hands of the most evil of them all, Briggs, who thought his anger and bitterness gave him the right to take another man's life, and possibly that of his own wife as well. It had been established that the blood on that hammer, though much degraded, was probably hers.

But thank God there were still good people in the world. He glanced at Leanne standing beside him, honest as the day was long, not too happy at the moment, but it would pass. He put his arm around her waist and drew her to him. He knew that his own weaknesses, especially his attraction towards pretty women, had almost caused domestic disaster, and he vowed to overcome this failing. And the twins, racing around on this hilltop, like the innocents they were. He knew it would be more and more difficult to keep them that way as they reached their teenage years, but he'd bloody well try. But he wasn't alone in his battle against increasing evil. There were good people like Jane, Patrick, Agnieska. Lesia, even Darren and of course his own wonderful sidekick, Dawn Eccles. But enough of all that introspection. Live each day as if it was your last, as Tony – another good man – would say.

On top of the hill stood a row of detached houses, in large gardens.

'Imagine living in one of those,' said Leanne. 'Bet they cost a fortune.'

They walked on along the path, at the edge of another field, until Sean suddenly announced, 'I'm hungry, Dad. Can we go to McDonald's now?'

'Just a bit further,' said Jack, and when they reached the end of that field, he turned and they made their way back towards the car. The walk had been really relaxing, and it had given him an idea.

Next morning Jack spent time in his little office looking something up online, then said that he had to go somewhere but would be back soon. Leanne sighed, thinking they wouldn't see him for ages, but after an hour or so she heard his car pull up on their short drive, with a quick toot of the horn. The twins rushed out to greet him and were puzzled when he carried a large cardboard box into the house.

'What's that, Dad?' asked Sean.

'It's a present for your mum, but you might be able to share it.'

His sister thought it might be something like a cake, but then she heard a strange noise coming from the box. Cakes didn't usually make strange noises.

Jack put the box carefully down on the floor and called Leanne.

At last she came into the hallway and saw the box.

'What on earth is that, Jack?'

It's a present for you. Go on, open it.'

Leanne bent down, lifted one flap of the box and squealed with delight. She lifted the other flap, put both hands into the box and drew out a little dog. The twins 'oohed' and 'aahed'.

'It's not the prettiest of dogs,' said Jack. 'I got it fom the rescue kennels. It was just the way he looked at me and sort of said, "Please take me". He's house trained and used to spending his days alone. But he'll need walking morning and night.'

'I'll do that' shouted Sean.

'Me too,' said his sister.

Jack looked at Leanne, who had lifted the little dog up to her face where it was nuzzling her right ear. He saw a huge smile on her face and knew he'd got it right this time.

FIFTY-FIVE

They had stayed overnight at the Crown Hotel, probably the best in the town. Jane had slept well and felt that she had really recovered from the dreadful events of the last few days. Patrick too seemed happier. He had his beloved car back. Preston was dead and his two evil accomplices were behind bars. Jane also felt much better physically. It was as if their recent adventures had toughened her up. The morning sickness had eased off and after a hot shower she was ready to face the day, whatever it might bring.

Patrick had agreed to accompany her to the churchyard and visit her parents' graves. He had never been there before and had no memory of the dreadful events that began when the body of a young woman had been found in her father's grave, just as he was about to be interred. Of course Patrick later became involved in the search for the headquarters of that sex-trafficking gang, using his technological skill to track those bastards to Brampton Manor and his expert knowledge of the security system to gain entry. He was with Dundee, Eccles and Peter Staines when they rescued Agnieska and, with the help of some armed policemen, ended the exploits of the infamous Lord Oxendale. It was during the gunfight with those criminals that Peter Staines had been shot and later died on the operating table. Peter's funeral had taken place in the same church they would be visiting that morning, but Patrick had not been there at the time.

It was probably Pete who first brought out Jane's maternal feelings. He was so young, not only in years, but in his thinking about life. He had been very stupid to get mixed up with her father and his misguided attempt to recapture his first love, which had led to Pete's disastrous involvement with the sex-trafficking gang in Spain. When he realised how naïve he had been, Pete did everything he could to put things right. Not only did he save the Spanish girl Felicia from that gang but then he came back to England with the intention of going to the police, admitting his part in the girl's death and telling them all he knew about the evil sex-trafficking scheme.

Jane had discovered Pete hiding in her father's house. She had taken him with her to Tony's mansion in Kent where he had told Jack and Dawn all he knew about the way the gang worked. Pete began to treat Jane like a mother, helping her in the kitchen, asking her advice and telling her about his feelings for Felicia. When Jack made his plan and asked Agnieska to infiltrate the headquarters of the gang, Pete went with them and met his untimely end.

After breakfast they packed their bags and set off. The village where Jane had spent her childhood lay just to the south of Bridgeport and they would continue their journey to London once they had made their brief stop at the church. The contrast with the day of her father's funeral was very apparent: then it had been cold, grey and wet, now the sun shone with early spring warmth.

They parked and climbed the steep flight of steps to the church. The clock in its ancient tower struck eleven. The rooks were quarrelling among the sycamores. Patrick and Jane walked round the church and down the slope towards the graves. The ground was drier this time and made walking much easier. When Jane reached her mother's grave she saw that it had been tidied up and flowers had been placed on it in a metal vase. Her mother had always been well liked in the village and someone had obviously visited the grave recently and left the flowers but these were now faded and drooping. Jane had always wondered what the point was of putting flowers on graves and yet she had felt a compulsion to do exactly that and had bought some fresh daffodils from the florist on the High Street. She lifted out the old flowers and asked Patrick to go up to the well beside the church and put fresh water in the vase. As he set off up the slope she turned to her father's grave. No one had cut the grass on his grave and there were no flowers or even an empty vase. She had had a simple stone erected with his name and dates, but someone had daubed a message on the stone 'Sex Maniac'. She had no means of rubbing away the graffiti and she thought perhaps it was almost justified. But looking at his grave she remembered the flowers which had been placed on it at the time of the funeral. One bunch had been from his publishers but no one from the firm had bothered to attend. The other, a very tasteful bouquet, was from someone called Tony.

She had never heard of Tony until that time but was soon to meet him and discover that he had spent his childhood with her father, though they had never seen one another since. Tony told her about the girl they had both loved in their teens and who had broken her father's heart.

Jane had discovered what a lovely man Tony was and wished that *he* could have been her father. It was at Tony's mansion in Kent that they had all stayed when they planned the attack on the sex traffickers. Tony had won the lottery and was now a rich man, though still down to earth and full of fun.

Jane remembered so clearly all of them sitting round Tony's table, while Jack outlined his plans: Agnieska bravely offering to infiltrate the gang, Patrick designing the tracker, Jack and Dawn Eccles preparing to unmask the leader of that gang and Peter Staines ready and willing to use his youth and strength in their support.

Tony and Jane were forced to stay in Kent and hope all went well. He was severely disabled and there was no room for Jane in the minibus in which they would make their chase. Patrick was not meant to go either but he had followed the minibus in his Porsche. In fact it was a good job that he had because he knew all about the Manor's security system having actually installed it a while ago. Jane remembered how she and Tony had walked anxiously around his garden waiting to hear how the plan had gone.

But where on earth was Tony? In the last few days she had tried to contact him several times but his phone was always dead. She longed to tell him about her pregnancy. He would be delighted. She worried that something may have happened to him. He was not a young man and liked his food and wine. He suffered from severe arthritis so he might have fallen and been taken to hospital. Once she was back in London she would begin to make some serious enquiries, perhaps even go down to Kent and find out what had happened to him.

Patrick returned with the vase full of water and she placed the daffodils on her mother's grave. He saw the graffiti on the next grave and was horrified.

'I've got some stuff in the car that will get rid of it.'

He set off up the slope again. Jane stood in the quiet churchyard and thought about her mother. She had always been so kind. Like most young people she had never really appreciated her mother when she was alive and wished she could thank her now and tell her how much she had loved her. She would have made a wonderful grandmother.

Patrick brought a small bottle and a rag and wiped away the words on the granite headstone. Jane reached up and gave him a hug. There was nothing else they could do, without proper gardening tools, to tidy the grave, so they walked back up to the church.

'Can we have a peep inside?' asked Patrick. 'I love these old churches.'

There was a wheelchair in the porch. Jane wondered how anyone in a wheelchair would get up all those steps, but then remembered Moira telling her that a lift had recently been built against the sandstone cliff on which the church stood, so that members of the congregation, many of whom were elderly and infirm, could get to the services.

The church door was open – quite a surprise these days – and Jane and Patrick stepped quietly inside. An elderly man and a young woman sat in the front pew near the chancel, looking towards the altar. There was something familiar about them both. Suddenly Jane realised exactly who they were and broke the silence as she hurried towards them.

'Tony! Felicia! What on earth are you doing here?'

Tony turned but didn't try to stand. He held up his arms saying, 'Jane. What a wonderful surprise. And Patrick too. What on earth brings you here?'

'I could ask you the same.'

Jane bent down to give Tony a hug. By now Felicia had stood up. Jane thought how lovely she looked, with her long dark hair in a ponytail and her dark features clearly outlined against her olive skin. No wonder Peter Staines had been so attracted to her. Almost his last words had been, 'Tell Felicia how much I love her.'

By now the young woman had stepped around Tony and stood in the aisle. Patrick kissed her on both cheeks, in the continental manner, then Felicia and Jane embraced like old friends. Felicia's English had improved a good deal since Jane had last seen her.

'I asked Tony to bring me here. It is the last place where I saw Pete. Though he was in his coffin by then. But I love this little church.'

Patrick announced, 'Look, folks, it's almost lunchtime. Why don't we find a local pub, order something to eat and catch up on all our news?'

Jane told them that there was a suitable pub quite near the church. They could walk there easily. And they served a good lunch. She had used it for her father's funeral, though after the discovery of the body in his grave she had missed out on that meal. She longed to tell Tony about her pregnancy, but suddenly felt very hungry. Her news could wait.

Tony managed to stand and, assisted by Felicia, walked down the aisle to the porch. The way she helped him into his chair and the way he touched her hand in gratitude made Jane wonder whether Tony's charm and Felicia's beauty had turned their friendship into something deeper. No, she dismissed that idea immediately. Tony was not such a fool.

Patrick took over the role of wheelchair pusher and Jane heard both men laughing as they descended in the lift. She and Felicia walked down to the pub together. Suddenly Felicia asked, 'Jane, there is something different about you.'

'Perhaps,' Jane said and smiled.

They reached the pub, called The Old Ferry, because there had once been a river crossing here, using the river's current to push a boat across the water, controlled by a wire stretched from bank to bank. The ferry had ceased to operate even before she was born, but Jane had seen a photograph of the ferry boat with its ancient ferryman on the wall of this very pub.

The pub was nearly empty, because it was a weekday and still quite early so they chose a corner table and ordered their food and drink. Jane could no longer remain silent. She announced, 'I have some good news. I'm pregnant.' She pointed at Patrick. 'And this is the father.'

Tony grabbed her hands and held them tight, 'Jane, that's brilliant news. I'm so pleased.'

'I've been itching to tell you for days, but you never seemed to be at home, and you didn't answer your phone.'

'Ah, well you see, while you and Patrick were gallivanting about and you were getting pregnant, Felicia and I have been having a little adventure of our own in Spain.'

Felicia seemed to shudder as he said this.

'Adventure?' asked Patrick. 'Tell us more.'

'Well,' said Tony, then paused, in true storyteller fashion. 'It began about a week ago, with a telephone call in the middle of the night...'

Acknowledgements

My thanks go to Reg Turrell for his great picture of Whixall Moss and to Helen Baggott for her skilful proof reading. I would also like to thank John Heap for completing the cover design and preparing the book for printing. Finally, my thanks go Leaf-by-Leaf Press for all their support in the making of the novel.

The author is a Shropshire lad. He attended Goldsmiths College in London, studying Speech and Drama. While there he wrote a one act play which won the London University One Act Play Festival and went on to win the South East England Festival. For many years writing had to take second place to providing for his family. When he retired from teaching he began to write again, including a full length play, produced locally, a story read on the radio and several prize winning poems. He has written two historical novels, one published on the internet, and is working on a third. 'Murder on the Moss' is his second contemporary crime novel.

Also by R. J. Turner

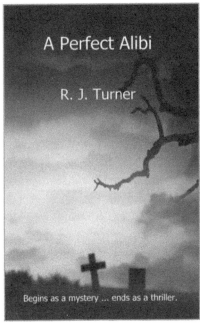

A Perfect Alibi

Richard Downs, an ageing, mid-list crime writer, suffers a severe stroke and dies in hospital, with his daughter at his bedside. She arranges his funeral, but when his coffin is about to be lowered into the grave a terrible discovery is made. During the investigation that follows, Jane begins to learn some horrid truths about her father.

'A thoroughly gripping tale from a writer who deserves a wider audience.'
Dave Andrews, author of 'The Oswestry Round' and the Himalayan journal 'Gobowen to Everest'.